5/13

More Critical Praise for Preston L. Allen

for *Jesus Boy*

"Heartfelt and occasionally hilarious, *Jesus Boy* is a tender masterpiece."
—Dennis Lehane, author of *Mystic River* and *The Given Day*

"Generations of illicit sex run through this clever and wide-ranging book [about religious addiction] in which the flesh always triumphs . . . Surely no one does church sexy like Allen . . . Allen's writing by turns is solemn and funny . . . It would be easy for *Jesus Boy* to become fluffy satire but Allen keeps his characters real."
—*New York Times Book Review*

"Allen has created a consummate tragicomedy of African American family secrets and sorrows, and of faith under duress and wide open to interpretation. Perfect timing and crackling dialogue, as well as heartrending pain balanced by uproarious predicaments, make for a shout-hallelujah tale of transgression and grace, a gospel of lusty and everlasting love."
—*Booklist*

"*Jesus Boy* is one of those books that makes you sit up and go . . . WHAT? No novel should be this enthralling. With a mesmerizing style, Preston L. Allen offers sentences that you reread because of their sheer enchantment and sense of wonder they invoke . . . in magical prose that lights up the pages. This is a novel unlike any I've ever read and among the very best of the decade. What a joy to read a book you can truly call a contemporary classic."
—Ken Bruen, author of *Sanctuary* and *The Guards*

"Ten More Titles to Read Now: Think African American Romeo and Juliet, as played out in a devout Christian community."
—*O, The Oprah Magazine*

"This latest from Allen is hilarious . . . Scenes of preaching and singing in the church convey the boisterous fervor of African American gospel music and

religious practice in a soulful, vibrant style . . . This is a very enjoyable and well-done novel; highly recommended."
—*Library Journal*

"A riveting story of star-crossed love, *Jesus Boy* plumbs the hypocrisies and impossible stringencies of evangelical America with humor and no small amount of pathos. This novel is definitely a guilty pleasure."
—Cristina García, author of *Dreaming in Cuban*

for *All or Nothing*

"As with Frederick and Steven Barthelme's disarming gambling memoir, *Double Down*, the chief virtue of *All or Nothing* is its facility in enlightening nonbelievers, showing how this addiction follows recognizable patterns of rush and crash, but with a twist—the buzz is in the process, not the result . . . As a cartographer of autodegradation, Allen takes his place on a continuum that begins, perhaps, with Dostoyevsky's *Gambler*, courses through Malcolm Lowry's *Under the Volcano*, William S. Burroughs's *Junky*, the collected works of Charles Bukowski and Hubert Selby Jr., and persists in countless novels and (occasionally fabricated) memoirs of our puritanical, therapized present. Like Dostoyevsky, Allen colorfully evokes the gambling milieu—the chained (mis)fortunes of the players, their vanities and grotesqueries, their quasi-philosophical ruminations on chance. Like Burroughs, he is a dispassionate chronicler of the addict's daily ritual, neither glorifying nor vilifying the matter at hand."
—*New York Times Book Review*

"Dark and insightful . . . The well-written novel takes the reader on a chaotic ride as . . . Allen reveals how addiction annihilates its victims and shows that winning isn't always so different from losing."
—*Publishers Weekly*

"A gambler's hands and heart perpetually tremble in this raw story of addiction. 'We gamble to gamble. We play to play. We don't play to win.' Right there, P, desperado narrator of this crash-'n'-burn novella, sums up the madness . . . Allen's brilliant at conveying the hothouse atmosphere of hell-bent gaming. Fun time in the Inferno."
—*Kirkus Reviews*

Every Boy Should Have a Man

Preston L. Allen

This is a work of fiction. All names, characters, places, and incidents are the product of the author's imagination. Any resemblance to real events or persons, living or dead, is entirely coincidental.

Published by Akashic Books

Hardcover ISBN-13: 978-1-61775-162-2
Paperback ISBN-13: 978-1-61775-157-8
Library of Congress Control Number: 2012954414

First printing

Akashic Books
PO Box 1456
New York, NY 10009
info@akashicbooks.com
www.akashicbooks.com

To Dawn, with love
in lesser darkness, in greater darkness, in brighter light that follows
ever by my side
ever holding my hand

Acknowledgments

Many thanks to my readers Ellen Milmed, Tiina Lombard, Edward Glenn, Jason Murray, William Durnell, and Kevin Eady, to my editor Ibrahim Ahmad, to my publisher Johnny Temple, to my agent Eleanor Jackson, and to the Earth Ethics Institute at Miami Dade College, whose class in the swamps inspired this book.

Much props, all.

Now consider the man. He does not overhunt. He does not overeat. Man is one with great nature. The oaf can learn much from the man. His sun rises in gold but sets in blood. His fire burns the world.

—Great Scripture

1

Every Boy Should Have a Man

He was not unusual because he had a man. In those days every boy had a man or wanted one.

He was not unusual because he had a man that talked. With the boom in mining and the approaching war, they were breeding more talking mans, and many boys—at least those born to well-to-do families—had mans that talked.

What made this boy unusual was that he was born to a poor family and he had a man that talked.

He was playing in the bramble after school one day when he spotted the man.

"A man!" the boy exclaimed.

The man said, "Hello there."

"A man that talks!" squealed the delighted boy.

He did not look like a wild or dangerous man, so the boy fashioned a leash out of string from his sack and led the man home.

He played with him in his room until just before his mother came home. He told the man, "Don't say anything or I will be punished."

The man, who seemed to have understanding, said, "Okay."

Then the boy put him under the bed.

The mother came home, and then the father. The man under the bed said nothing, and the evening ended with night as it always did.

In the morning before the boy left for school, he checked under his bed.

"I'm hungry," said the man.

"Hungry?"

"At the place where I was before, they fed me."

"What do you eat?"

"I don't know. What do *you* eat?"

The boy went out into the kitchen and brought back his meager breakfast which his mother had left for him and gave it to the man. The boy watched as the man ate. The man ate everything. The boy's hungry stomach growled as he watched.

The man looked up from the plate he had licked clean. "Now I'm thirsty."

The boy came back with water and watched as the man drank. Then he put the man back under the bed and left for school.

After school the boy raced home and checked under his bed. The man's snore was a steady buzz. The boy shook him until his eyes drooped open.

"Come on, let's play."

"I'm hungry again."

"Uh . . . okay."

The man followed as the boy checked the house for food. Sometimes when the boy turned, the man would be inspecting some object in his hand—Mother's prized glass bowl, a dish towel, the shiny tin of cooking oil, the small singing harp—and the boy would invariably order the man to put the thing down and he would do so obediently, for he was an obedient man.

Opening a cupboard, the boy discovered the scraps of meat his mother had hung to dry. The man took them from him and devoured them quickly. But afterward he was playful and talkative. All in all, the boy was having a good time, though he worried what would happen when his parents found the scraps of meat were missing.

Just before it was time for his parents to arrive home, the boy put the man back under the bed and prepared for the worst.

His mother would be wroth. She would scold and threaten with punishments severe. But he would stand his ground. He would cry, "But Mom, every boy should have a man. All the other kids have one. Why can't I? It's just not fair."

Maybe it would work. Maybe.

That evening when his parents arrived home, they were in a grand mood, having stopped off at the festival and come back with sacks full of food. At the festival there is much food and everyone is free to eat. No one is supposed to eat to excess or put the food in sacks and take it home, but his parents were known to be poor and so the authorities, as usual, looked the other way.

The evening became night, the boy's mother did not mention the missing scraps of dried meat, and the boy went to bed believing that he had gotten away with it.

Under the bed, his man was talking. He was saying silly things and singing silly songs: "Fly me to the moon. Fly me to the stars. Fe, fe, fe! Victory!" The words made no sense, but the boy listened, enchanted, until he fell asleep.

The next day, the boy raced home after school to be with his man, but he found his mother fussing around the kitchen—his mother, who almost never came home early. Before the boy could say a word, his mother scolded, "Let me see this man of yours."

The boy was frightened speechless. Mother didn't look angry, not exactly, but she continued to scold: "What have you been feeding him? All of our food? I was saving that meat. They don't eat that. He's going to get sick and make a big mess. When your father finds out, what do you think he's going to say? You know his temper. You didn't steal this man, did you?"

He led her into his room and bid the man come out from under the bed.

The man emerged timidly. First his head popped out, then his limbs. Unfolding himself, he stood to his full height. He was tall—almost as tall as the boy. He was a tall man, but thin. His ribs showed through his skin. He hadn't been eating properly since even before the boy had found him, and they lose weight so fast when they do not eat.

His hair was matted with dirt, bramble, and what appeared to be bird droppings. He smelled like feces. He looked like a well-bred man, so the mother didn't imagine that he had messed on himself—but she knew that somewhere under the bed was a pile of his droppings that she would have to locate and remove before the whole place smelled like a zoo.

The boy's mother took the man out back and washed him down with soapy water and a sponge. The man shivered as she dried his body with the fluffy towel Grandmother had given them. He had brownish skin, with areas around his elbows and knees darker than everywhere else.

She scratched his head with one of her combs, and when she had the hairs on his head under control, she tied the ends of them with little bits of colored cloth. She trimmed the coarse hairs on his chest and loins with clippers of brass, and then she pinched his loins into a crisp red pouch retrieved from her room.

The man was very pretty after the mother was done with him—him with his new hair cloths and fancy loin pouch. He looked like the man of a wealthy family now and this troubled her.

The mother went out to the market and returned with some vegetables and grains. She explained to the boy: "This is what they eat."

"But he ate all the meat that I gave him. He seemed to like it."

The mother shook her head. "They are not *cannibals*. Eating of his own flesh will make him sick."

She set the food in a bowl before the man, and she and the boy watched as he ate. He was a well-trained man, who ate without spilling. As the man ate, the boy petted his head and the mother, caught up in nostalgia, told him, "I had a man when I was a little girl."

"I love my man," the boy said, playfully pinching the man's ear as he chewed his food.

"He's a very fine man, indeed," the mother observed. "I loved my man too, when I was a little girl. But my father, your grandfather, he didn't like him at all." The mother spoke in a calm, sad voice. "When I was about your age, I got my man. We found three little mans aimlessly wandering around the schoolyard. Juveniles with no adult that we could see. They were part of a litter, we guessed, but they did not all look alike. Two were pale and stout—one was brown, and he was tall like this one, though not so handsome. The teacher decided to put our names in a hat. The first name she drew was mine. I chose the brown one. He had dark brown skin and coal-black eyes. Because there was a lighter spot on his cheek, I called him *Bright Cheek*. I brought him home on a leash that the teacher gave me. My mother took one look at him and shook her head. *Your father is not going to like this one bit*, she warned. But I begged and pleaded, so she cleaned him up, fed him, and then sewed pretty cloths for his hair and a pouch for his loins. That same one there that your man is wearing." She pointed to the pretty red pouch. "Then we placed some bedding on the ground so that he would have a place to sleep. When my father came home and saw the man, he started yelling right away and did not stop until the morning. *No mans! I hate mans, they are messy and smelly and they carry diseases!* he kept yelling. I cried and cried. The only reason he resisted throwing the man out into the street that night was because it was stormy and there was a law about cruelty to mans. When morning came your grandmother got up and prepared the man, and she helped me take him back to school. The teacher put the names in the hat again, all except mine, and I watched as another girl won my man and took him home. I cried and cried."

"I'm not going to let Father give my man away!" the boy shouted.

"Well, we'll just have to keep him under the bed until I can talk to your father. I'll try to talk to him."

"I'm not going to let Father give him away! I'm not going to let anybody take him. I'm going to keep him forever and ever," said the boy, with the resoluteness of an innocent. "And I'm going to call him *Brown Skin!*"

The boy hugged the man's neck as he spoke. The man gazed up at the boy with what could pass for understanding. The mother noticed and a horrified expression appeared on her face. She said to the boy, "Can he talk? Is he a man that talks?"

The boy, who was usually very honest, saw the look on his mother's face and told a small lie: "No. He can't talk."

The mother seemed to relax after that, her pleasant smile returning, and she began to pet the man, who was already being hugged and petted by the boy. The mother was smiling, but she muttered under her breath and mostly to herself a warning: "Only the wealthy own mans that talk. We don't need that kind of trouble."

It went well for two more days, days in which the boy played with his man that he kept under the bed, and the mother considered different approaches for talking to the father about the secret guest in their house.

On the third day, the boy, overcome by an adventurous spirit, decided to take the man out for a walk. He warned the man not to talk, of course, and the man agreed. He was a man with very good understanding.

They went to the market. They went to the square. They went to the field where other boys—the sons of wealthy families—were walking their mans. Everywhere they went, the boy received compliments for having such a fine, handsome, pleasant-smelling man.

Then they went to the green hill where boys were flying kites and workers were setting up for the next festival.

The mayor, who had come to inspect, was there with his wife. But the mayor was no expert on festivals: another election was coming and he was really there to collect votes.

The mayor's wife, an avid lover of mans, spotted the boy and his man and came straightway over and announced: "That is a fine man you have there!"

The boy, who was enjoying all the attention, did not detect the false appreciation in her voice and answered boastfully, "Yes, he is a fine man. He is the finest man in the world!"

"Where does he get such fine bright cloths for his hair?"

"My mother made them. She is clever with her hands," the boy said. "She makes all of our clothes too."

"And does your man speak?" the mayor's wife asked, her voice at last revealing her true emotion, anger. "Does your clever-handed mother make fine conversation with your man that talks?"

"No," the boy heard his mouth say. "He does not talk."

The mayor's wife held him firmly by the shoulder and shook him as she spoke: "And from where did your clever mother *steal* this man that talks?"

"My mother did not steal him," said the boy, pulling against her firm grip. He wanted to run away. He wanted to run far away from there.

But the mayor's wife gripped him ever more tightly. "From where did your clever mother steal *my* man that talks?"

"He doesn't talk. She didn't steal him," the boy stammered.

"We'll see about that."

Now there was a big commotion, and a crowd had gathered—the boys with their kites, the workers with their tools, and even the mayor bustled over.

The mayor proved to be more civil than his wife, because he did not want to scare off any potential votes from among the gathered workers, but the law is the law and theft of property is against the law. His wife, who still had a firm grip on the boy, had so many of them at home that she did not actually recognize this one as the man that had gone missing a month and a half ago, but the man could talk and the boy was obviously poor. That was evidence enough. It did not help that the man kept shouting at intervals, "I want to stay with the boy forever and ever!"

So his mother was called for.

At this point the boy was admitting that the man was not his, because he did not want to get his mother in trouble. He admitted that he had found the man wandering in the bramble.

But the mayor's wife was demanding justice. There was talk of arrest and punishments severe.

The boy's mother became distraught. The mayor, again trying to resolve things in a civil fashion, sent for the boy's father.

The father appeared wearing the uniform of his labor with his head hung low. The father wore the uniform of a loader.

The mayor's wife was issuing threats in a voice that had become hoarse from shouting, the mother was weeping softly with her hand on the boy's head, and the boy was holding the man's hand, or rather the man was clutching the boy's hand and repeating, "I like the boy. I want to stay with the boy forever and ever. I like the boy. I like his mother too."

The mayor pulled the father away from the throng and addressed him: "Do you understand what is going on here?"

The father answered sadly, "Yes, I do, sir."

"My wife has every right, you know?"

The father sighed, "Yes, I know she does."

"Do you have any idea the trouble you and your family are in if she pursues this? And you are completely in the wrong on this."

The father nodded hopelessly, the worry lines on his face multiplying.

"But," the mayor whispered, "she does tend to blow things out of proportion."

"Does she?" asked the father.

The mayor pressed a finger to a dirt-caked button on the father's uniform. "Now, we have an election coming up. There are big things that I would like to do. Big things for everyone. And I need votes. Everyone's votes. Yours. Your neighbors'. Your fellow loaders'. I have big plans for everyone, but my wife—she blows everything completely out of proportion."

The mayor put a hand on the father's back, and turning, they faced the mother, the mayor's wife, the boy, and his man. The mouth of the mayor's wife was still flapping, but now they all looked exhausted, even the man, who kept repeating, "I like the boy. I like his mother too."

"Now your boy—he looks like a fine boy. I believe him when he says he found the man. Who would be so unwise as to steal a man from *her*?" joked the mayor. "Her mans run off all the time. She has too many of them. She loves them to death but she can't keep track of them. Frankly, I think she talks so much she scares them off."

When the mayor laughed, it was a politician's laugh, a laugh that put everyone at ease. The father, at ease now, laughed along with the mayor, whose hand was still on his back.

The mayor said to him, "Go home, you and your family. No harm was done. The man looks healthy enough. Your boy took good care of him. You have a fine boy there."

"Thank you, sir."

"You're a union man, aren't you?"

"Well, yes, sir. I am."

"Good! I'm all for that. Talk to your fellows. I sure could use their vote."

They walked home in silence, the father, the mother, and the boy.

The boy could only imagine the great embarrassment he had caused his father—how terribly the mayor must have scolded him. He could only imagine the elaborate punishments that awaited. In his little hands were the pretty red pouch and the colored cloths his man had worn; in his heart, there was only sorrow.

When they got home, the father said nothing to the boy.

At mealtime, it was a good meal, made up of the excess they had taken from the festival. The father was still wearing his unwashed loader's uniform—he never wore his uniform at the table, but he said nothing. He ate his meal in silence. The mother and the boy—they ate their meals in silence.

After mealtime it was evening, and evening turned to night in the silent home.

The wealthy do not understand the sorrows of the poor. The poor do not understand the sorrows of the wealthy. Another war would come soon.

That night in the home of the poor loader, the boy dreamt of a great festival that went on and on forever, and everybody had a man.

In the morning the boy went to school, and when he came home his mother was home from work early again.

He worried that something was wrong—that he had done something wrong again—but the sadness he had seen on her face the day before was gone and she was cheerful. He nevertheless was suspicious because it was not like her to be home at such an early hour.

When he got to his room, he jumped for joy. There was a man on his bed!

It was not as big as the man he had found that had run away from the mayor's loud wife, nor was it as fine looking.

Later he would learn that it was also *not* a man that talked.

Nor was it one that was bred for the mines.

Nor was it a man that only a wealthy family could afford.

It was just an average run-of-the-mill man, and he loved her already. He ran and threw his arms around her neck.

It was a female man.

It was a female man with colored cloths in her hair, the red pouch covering her loins, and a note tied up in the red ribbon around her neck.

As his smiling mother looked on through the doorway, the boy opened his father's note and read the words which retold an eternal truth: *Every boy should have a man. You're a fine son. Love, Father.*

2
His Female Man

And the boy was happy with his man.

His man was fast. She could outrun all the other mans in the neighborhood.

His man was a good fighter. She could lick any other man in the neighborhood, but he did not let her fight too often because his mother did not approve of man-fights, which were considered by many to be cruelty to mans. His mother would be so angry after a fight that she would threaten to give his man away if he fought her again.

His man was loyal. She went everywhere he went and cried every morning as he left for school.

His man was ferocious. She showed her teeth whenever a stranger came too near him. To calm her, he would pet her head and kissy-coo her. "Down, girl, down," he would kissy-coo until she became calm, and even then she would keep one eye on the stranger. His man did not trust strangers.

And though she was a man that could neither talk nor sing, she was a musically gifted man, they discovered, when she picked up

Mother's small singing harp one day and began to pluck the strings.

At first they were amused that the female man was trying to make the harp sing. The singing harp is a difficult instrument to play, even for someone like Mother who had had music lessons as a child, but after a few moments of amusement and mirth, Mother exclaimed, "Wait, I know that song! I know what she's trying to play."

She got up from her knitting, took the singing harp from the man, and plucked a few strings to show them, and the harp sang: "In the heart, in the air, hear the joy everywhere . . ."

Of course, they all knew the song. They had all learned it as children. They sang the song along with the singing harp that Mother played and gazed in wonder at their female man.

But then the father said, "Maybe it was just coincidence. I know nothing about music, and sometimes when I touch the harp in passing, I will hear something that reminds me of a song I know. Give it back to her and see if she can do it again."

So they gave her back the harp, and the female man set her fingers against the strings. They leaned toward her with expectation. She looked at them with innocent eyes. She had bright green eyes and fine red body hair. There were frecks of rusty-red color on her face and her shoulders and all across her chest, above and below her teats, and her arms were covered with rusty-red frecks, like rusty-red sleeves on a shirt. And that is why the boy named her *Red Sleeves*.

"Play it," said the boy, petting her. "Play. Show them."

She looked at him with her mouth open. There were a few tiny frecks above and below her lips too.

The mother urged, "Come on, girl."

They waited and waited.

Leaning back in his comfortable chair and hiding his knowing smile behind the day's paper again, the father let out a laugh. They heard him say: "Coincidence."

"Play," said the boy. "Come on, girl, play."

"Maybe she's hungry," said the mother. "Maybe she'll play if she eats something." She got up and went into the kitchen.

"Play," kissy-cooed the boy.

From behind his paper, the father said, "She's a good fighter, though. If your mother wasn't so set against it, I know someone, a professional, who could train her, then we could enter her in the big fights at the festival. Against what they've got, she would place at least third."

The boy said, "First place! She can lick anybody's stinky old man." The boy kissy-cooed, "Come on, girl, play for me. Show them you can do it."

They waited and waited.

The father lowered his paper and said to the boy, "Money is important, and she is but a man. If you earn money from making an animal do what it does naturally, how is that cruel? She is a good fighter."

"The best!" cried the boy.

"Yes," said the father, "and she should be allowed to fight! If we didn't tell your mother, maybe we could sneak off to the—"

But the mother came back from the kitchen with a snack for the man. A big leafy stick of green vegetable. The man took the vegetable and devoured it.

"Play," said the boy, rubbing the man's stomach. "Show them you can play."

The father chuckled smugly—a man of the poor does not play music. The mother, still hopeful, leaned in close for almost a minute and, when nothing happened, she went back to her chair next to the father where she had left her knitting.

And suddenly the singing harp began to sing: "In the heart, in the air, hear the joy everywhere. Shall we call, shall we sing, of the joy everywhere . . ."

The boy clapped and laughed excitedly. "See? I told you!"

The mother said, "Whoever owned her before must have taught her to do it."

The father nodded. "She knows all the words. She's better than the trained man at the circus. She must be worth good money."

"Whoever owned her before must have sat with her and trained her. Where did you get her?"

"She was a take-in. The kennel boss said her owners practically gave her away. But they were poor."

"How old is she?"

"Her license says she's fifteen."

"In man years?"

"She was born five years ago, it says, so yes, she's fifteen in man years."

The mother got up and went over to the female man playing the singing harp and watched with fascination the nimble movements of the rusty-red-frecked fingers as the instrument sang, "In the heart, in the air, hear the joy everywhere, in the heart, in the heart, in the heart . . ."

The mother exclaimed, "That's the way my music teacher taught me to play it! Repeat the *heart* part three times." She rubbed the man's head. "I don't think she's stolen. Sometimes the take-ins are stolen. Do you think she's stolen?"

The father said, "She didn't cost much."

"Maybe they were trying to get rid of her because she was stolen," suggested the mother. "Only the wealthy can afford a musical man."

The father folded the paper in his lap. "Maybe they didn't know she was musical. Maybe that's why they sold her so cheap. They didn't know. Her license looks real. It's not easy to forge a man license, is it?"

They both looked at the man playing the singing harp and at the boy who was staring up at them with worried eyes. The mother inhaled a deep breath. "Well, she may be stolen. What are we going to do?"

The father got up and patted the boy on the head. "She's ours now, and we're going to keep it like that. We just won't tell anybody that she is a musical man."

The boy smiled, the mother let out a relieved breath, and the father squatted on the ground with his family and listened enraptured as the female man made the small singing harp sing. The father patted the man's head and mused, "She must be worth some good money."

The female man knew ten songs that they remembered from their early childhood, and she played them one after the other, and they were all very happy.

* * *

When the boy would take his man out for a walk, he would try to follow his mother's wishes and avoid the field where the boys from wealthy families walked their mans, but sometimes the temptation was too great.

His man was the best fighter and the wealthy boys, showing off their expensive talking mans in their fabulous hair cloths and fancy loin pouches, needed to be taught a lesson that only the biggest, bravest, strongest, most ferocious man in the whole wide world could teach.

The rules were simple. No leashes. No biting. No gang-ups.

The boy, like a proud but bored spectator who has seen it all before, lay on his side with his head propped up on an elbow as the action proceeded.

His female man had already beaten six of them in a row, and this last one was about to cry surrender. She had this last one by the neck. She could snap his neck easily if she wanted, but she was content to hold his neck under one arm and punch him in the face with her free hand. The boy knew he should head back home before his mother began to worry, but he hated to call a fight in the middle, especially a slaughter like this.

He would make up an excuse to tell his mother.

While all around him the wealthy boys shouted encouragement to the doomed combatant, the poor boy arose from his place on the ground, stretched, yawned theatrically, and smirked. Nobody ever hooted and cawed for his man. Even though she was the best, she was a man of the poor. But this would teach them a lesson.

Six in a row and soon to be seven.

His man was punching the face of the man of the wealthy boy. The face of the wealthy boy's man was puffy and red. The female man landed two more hard blows, and the face of the wealthy boy's man dripped tears now as well as blood.

That was enough. The wealthy boy tapped the poor boy on the shoulder. "We surrender."

The poor boy said, "No. *He* has to say it."

The female man landed another hard blow and two teeth jumped from the mouth of the wealthy boy's man.

"But maybe he can't talk," said the wealthy boy to the poor. "He gets frozen when he's scared and he can't talk! We surrender!"

The poor boy snorted. "All right, girl. Let him up."

She released the wealthy boy's man and he fell on his face crying out, "Thank you for sparing my life."

As his victorious female man came running over to him, the poor boy turned to the wealthy boy and laughed. "See? He *can* talk. He's not frozen at all."

The wealthy boy, who was bigger than the poor boy, stepped toward him. "You think that's funny?"

The rest of them balled their fists and stepped toward the poor boy too.

The poor boy's female man showed her teeth and hissed at them dangerously, and they stepped back.

The poor boy laughed. "Watch out. She gets angry when people I don't like get too near."

The wealthy boys and their beaten mans took another step back.

As the poor boy and his female man departed for home, they heard bad names being shouted at them.

Bully!

Poor boy!

Cheater, cheater!

Pinhead!

Pinhead oaf!

The boy turned his head to show them the big smile on his face and to pink his tongue at them, but really it made him sad to be called such things. He was not a bully or a cheater—his man was just better than everybody else's. And he couldn't help it if his parents were poor. They were still the greatest parents in the whole wide world.

He ran so that he could get away from the things they were shouting. He ran until he heard a different sound, which was music.

At the far end of the field, only minutes away from his neighborhood and home, there was another boy—a wealthy boy—sitting on the grass while his mans, three of them, sang to him.

Each man had a different appearance, so the poor boy guessed that they were not from the same litter. The first man was tall and brown with hair that grew in a circle around his head, the second was shorter with a very round belly and his skin was pale, and the third was short and round and pale like the second, but his brown eyes were large and nearly lidless. All three of them wore blue cloths in their hair and matching blue loin pouches. They were three little man mans in blue.

The three mans were singing in a way that was very pleasing

to the ear. It was like the trained mans he had once seen at a circus, the way they sang. One voice was high-pitched, another was low, and the last was somewhere in between. Their song was very beautiful.

The wealthy boy did not seem arrogant or mean, so the poor boy sat down on the grass next to him and listened to the beautiful song of the singing mans in blue.

His female man seemed quite affected by the music; her eyes were closed as she listened, and her hips moved back and forth. The boy shouted a command, and she sat, but even while sitting, her hips continued to move.

The wealthy boy smiled at the female man. "She likes it. Maybe she is in heat."

The poor boy said, "What is *in heat*?"

"I'm not sure," the wealthy boy said, "but I used to have a female man who acted that way when they sang, and my parents said she was in heat. And then they had her fixed."

"What is *fixed*?"

"I don't know," laughed the wealthy boy. "But after she came back, she cried every time they sang. I think it has something to do with babies."

"Babies?"

The wealthy boy pointed to her moving hips. "She's a female man. She can have baby mans."

The poor boy hadn't thought of that, but he liked the idea.

"She's the best fighter in the whole world. She'll have lots of fighting baby mans."

The wealthy boy nodded. "I saw her fight. She's very good."

The poor boy nodded. "She's the best in the world."

"Is she going to fight at the circus?"

"My father wants her to, but my mother says no."

"She should fight. She's good. She would win."

"She beat seven in a row today. She beat them bloody. She knocked their teeth out. But my mother says it is cruel."

The wealthy boy grinned. "Yes, I saw it."

"Would you like her to fight one of your mans?" the poor boy offered.

The singing mans had stopped singing for some time now, and two of them were sitting on the grass listening as the boys talked.

The wealthy boy shook his head. "No, no, no, these are not fighting mans. These mans are very delicate. The circus pays us to have them sing."

The poor boy laughed and said, "Coward." But he said it in a way that was friendly and not mean.

"My sensitive and delicate little mans would be eaten alive if they tried to fight yours," laughed the wealthy boy.

"She would eat them for lunch," laughed the poor boy.

"I didn't know mans were cannibals." The wealthy boy snorted with mirth.

"She only eats sensitive and delicate singing mans dressed in blue," kidded the poor boy. Then he said, "Where is your other man? Isn't one of your mans missing?"

The poor boy was right. The one with the lidless eyes was missing.

And the wealthy boy asked the poor, "Where is *your* man?"

The poor boy turned to the empty space beside him. His female man was gone.

A short distance away, concealed by the rise of a low hill, their two missing mans were found, but entangled in such a way as the poor boy had never seen. The pale-skinned man in blue with the nearly lidless eyes was riding the back of his female man, who was emitting a rhythmic, shushy breath through her mouth.

The poor boy asked, "What are they doing?"

"I don't know," replied the wealthy boy, "but I don't like it. I think she's hurting him."

"But he's on top."

They watched for a few more seconds until the man with the lidless eyes contorted and began to groan. The female man closed her eyes and yelped, burying her face in the grass.

The two boys had seen enough. They shouted harsh commands and spanked their mans, separating them.

Then they replaced their loin pouches, said goodbye to each other, and went each to his own home.

That evening, the boy was wroth with his female man.

When she came to him with big, apologetic eyes, he shook his head. When she came to him and rested her head on his chest the way she did when she wanted to be petted, he pushed her away.

When she brought the small singing harp into his room, he said, "Okay, girl, you want to be friends again? Okay. Good girl."

And in the boy's bedroom his female man played the small singing harp and made it sing. He did not know why, but she was playing the same song over and over. He did not recognize the tune, though it was beautiful and vaguely familiar.

Evening became night, and eventually the boy fell asleep.

It was only the next day, as he was on his way to school, that the boy realized the song that she had been playing was the song he had heard the three mans in blue singing earlier that day at the field.

She began to change after that, but the boy did not notice until a month later.

Her diet had shifted. She was eating more often—she was stealing their food. She would even steal a piece of dried meat from the cupboard once in a while, which was cannibalism. She was gaining weight.

He took her to the field on a day when there was no school, and she lost two fights in a row.

He found a stick and spanked her with it to make her fiercer. He made her growl and show her teeth. He sent her into two more fights and she lost them both. Four in a row. That had never happened before.

"Maybe you're sick," he told her as he walked home holding her hand. Her eye bruised, her nose leaking blood, she was too exhausted to flinch when they were pelted with pebbles and provoked with jibes and hoo-haws by the wealthy boys who had triumphed at last over the poor boy and his mighty champion.

As tears spilled from her emerald eyes, the boy promised her, "You're sick, but when you feel better we'll be back. We'll teach those guys a lesson."

Yet her tears kept falling. He had never seen her like this.

He gave her what he thought was ample time to heal—a week—and he took her to fight again. But she had lost all interest in fighting and refused to do it.

He spanked her with the stick to make her fiercer, he even poked her with the stick, but she let the other mans pummel and scratch her flesh until she was shedding blood along with her tears. She would not lift a hand to her own defense. Each time the boy was forced to stop it by crying surrender. It was another bad day at the fights. She lost three in a row that day.

The wealthy boys cackled with glee and pinked their tongues rudely as the poor boy walked his badly beaten fighting man home in a hail of pebbles and hoo-haws.

And she was playing the small singing harp every evening in his room—the same song the three singing mans in blue had sung that day at the field.

When he went into the backyard to feed her one morning before school, she was not there.

He went to her sleeping tent under her favorite tree, and she was not there. He went back into the house to look for her because on evenings when it was cold, she would come inside and sleep under his bed or under the couch in the grand room near the fire. He looked everywhere in the house, and she was not there.

He said to himself, *Now, I hope she didn't jump the fence again.*

Puzzled, he went back outside, and she was in her tent as if she'd been there all along.

She was grateful for her food, which she devoured, and then she held out her bowl to him for more. He replenished her bowl with vegetables and grain, and as he watched her eat, he said, "I see you're very hungry. I guess you jumped the fence to go look for food. Don't do that. The authorities will pick you up. You'll get in trouble. If you're hungry, come into the house and wake me. Okay?"

To make her understand, he knocked on the wooden fence that ran the perimeter of their backyard and shook his head.

"Don't go over the fence," he repeated. "Obey me. Obey me."

The next morning when he went to feed her before school, he caught her climbing down the fence and ducking into her tent. She had just returned from wherever it was she roamed at night.

He spanked her and scolded her harshly. When he set out her food, she still had tears in her eyes, but he was at the end of his patience.

"You're going to get us in trouble! Don't force me to tie you up or lock you in the house!" He pounded the wooden fence. "Don't go over the fence! I know you understand! Obey me! Obey me!"

She stared at him blankly, then went back to her food.

He went into the house and came back out with an extra bowl of food and set it beside the first. "Now give me a hug," he said to her.

He held open his arms and she came for her hug. He lifted her for her hug. *She is getting so heavy*, he thought.

"You're my best friend in the whole world, you know?" He kissed her cheek, petted her head, and set her back on the ground.

She looked at him with perfect understanding.

She went back to her food and he left for school.

When the boy got home from school that day, his mother had left a note: *Meet me at the kennel.*

He checked the backyard. His female man was gone. He threw down his school sack and ran to the kennel.

They had put his female man in a large cage with several other mans.

She was not the only female, but she was the biggest of the dozen or so mans in there, most of whom were screaming wildly at the top of their lungs or running around in circles like mad mans.

One man, a pale talking one with dark sun spots burned into his cheeks, was proclaiming over and over, "I didn't do it. I would never ever do it. Please believe me."

His female man ran to the front of the cage as soon as she saw the boy and he reached through the bars and petted her on the head. "It's going to be okay, girl. Don't worry. Mother and I will get you out of here."

The boy turned to watch his mother, who stood a few paces away talking to the boss of the kennel.

The kennel boss had a long oval face and eyes that were set far apart. He was munching a green leafy vegetable as he talked to the boy's mother. The mother was doing a lot of head shaking as her mouth opened and closed. The kennel boss inhaled another large green leaf into his mouth and crunched it between large, crooked teeth.

"It's out of my hands," he explained to the mother. "When the man becomes a danger to society, then the law has to step in."

"I assure you," said the mother, "this is all a misunderstanding. She is the most gentle of creatures. She is well mannered and well trained. She is a danger to no one. Mans get out of their yards all the time and wander. It is their nature. This is no reason for them to be destroyed."

The boy grabbed his female man's hand through the bars of the cage when he heard that. *Destroyed.*

The leaf-munching kennel boss raised a finger. "I never spoke that word. I only said that putting her down is one of the options, and not even the most desirable or most likely of options. It all depends on the injured party—whether or not they want to pursue it. But the charges are serious. A home was broken into. A child was bitten."

The boy reached his arms into the cage and hugged his man. *A child was bitten.*

"You see," said the mother, "it's words like that that scare me. We love our man, and I assure you that she is incapable of doing the things you claim she has done."

The kennel boss shoved the entire vegetable into his mouth and it made a crunching sound. "I simply read the record to you, ma'am."

"But she is incapable of—"

"Ma'am, I know all the old sayings—*Train your man to be playful with children, but cross with thieves. There is no creature more loyal than a man. A happy man is a well-fed man, but a cross man keeps the home free of sneak thieves. Every boy should have a man.* I don't mean to sound insensitive, but you are like so many owners of mans. You are incapable of seeing him for what he is. Man is a predator, first and foremost. He is but good at two things: hunting and making baby mans. He is a predator. He is a carnivore. That's right. He is no different from us. And don't look down at me because I do this job, ma'am—I have degrees in animal science. Times are hard, so I must work here, but I am no pinheaded oaf. I have seen the studies. We keep mans from eating meat because we fear what they'll do if they get a taste for it. Remember, ma'am, we are meat too. I know some of them have interesting talents and they make good pets, but truth be told they are wild beasts and should be left to roam the forests for us to hunt. It wasn't too long ago that they were our top food source. You don't look wealthy—I bet you eat your fill of man, right? The meat is plentiful, inexpensive, and tasty. I love to eat man, though I don't want man to eat me or my children. But the wealthy—oh, they want us to protect man, to bring him into our homes as pets, to hug him. Oh, they say that it is the great creator's will that we give up eating meat altogether, they say it is the great creator's will that we all turn vegetarian. Vegetables are nice—I like vegetables just fine. But man is meat and meat is good to eat," he said with a loud crunch. "Like my mother used to tell me, *Stop playing with your food and eat him*." The kennel boss grinned.

The mother said, "You are a stupid oaf."

"We'll see who is the stupid oaf when the injured party gets here," came the muttered retort.

The kennel boss picked up a brass cup and slurped whatever liquid was in it and gargled it to help suck free the strands of green from the vegetable that had gotten stuck in his ugly teeth. The mother turned away in disgust.

"Don't worry," the boy comforted his man, "Mother and I will free you."

The boy hugged his female man through the bars, and the frantic little man man proclaiming his innocence ran over to them and grabbed one of the boy's hands and kissed it. "I didn't do it, kind sir. They have the wrong man. You and Mother must free me too. You must. You must."

Just then the kennel boss came over and rattled the cage noisily with the brass cup, and when the frantic man didn't back away from the bars, the kennel boss reached in and slammed the cup against his head.

Pock!

The frantic man released the boy's hand and retreated to the safety of the center of the cage, holding his head and crying, "It is a lie. I didn't do it. I didn't do it."

The kennel boss said to the boy, "Take your hands out of the cage, boy. They may look pretty, but some of these mans will snap your fingers off." He pointed to the frantic man proclaiming his innocence in the center of the cage. "That one there maimed his master, a boy about your age. Chewed two of his fingers clean off. Don't let him fool you. His kind has a reputation for turning on you. Now scoot. Get away from that cage."

The boy ran to his mother, who put her arms around him. "It'll be okay."

Tears rolled out of the boy's eyes. "She didn't do it, Mother."

The mother kissed him on the head and assured, "All will be well once the injured party gets here."

* * *

In walked a wealthy boy wearing expensive clothes and his equally well-dressed father.

As he walked past the mother, the kennel boss sneered, "At last, they're here. The injured party."

The wealthy boy and his father lingered at the display cages at the front of the kennel, pointing at this or that man with sighs and hoo-hahs of amazement at the sheer beauty and diversity of them. And indeed, they were beautiful and diverse. In color, they ranged from the crystalline pale of a sea bell to the golden yellow-brown of a burnt meat stick. In size and shape, some were longish and thin, others smallish and thickset. In countenance, some were peppered with frecks, some with birthmarks and sunspots, others unstained. And their noses! They were generously bulbous, impertinently pointed, gallantly winged, impudently pugged, or nobly sloping like an oaf's. One had a face so normal-looking that but for his size, he could have walked near undetected in a crowd.

The wealthy boy pointed to this one with a gleeful utterance. The wealthy father asked the kennel boss to open the cage, and with keys a-jangling, the kennel boss did so.

Observing this, the mother felt better about their prospects for a happy resolution. *Luck is on our side*, she thought. *The injured parties are lovers of man.*

Then her son exclaimed, pointing to the wealthy boy, "I know him!"

"Where do you know him from?" asked the mother.

"From the field. He has three singing mans. He is my friend."

"What were you doing at the field after I told you not to go back there? Man-fighting again, after I told you not to?"

"Yes, Mother," the boy quietly admitted.

"Well," she said, "maybe it will work out."

The boy and his mother watched as the kennel boss removed the selected man from its cage, leashed it, and filled out the forms and had the father of the wealthy boy sign in various places. To complete the transaction, there was an exchange of silver.

"I just love mans," they heard the wealthy father say with a laugh. "And we already have so many of them at home."

The mother and the boy waited patiently, not wanting to behave impertinently, and so it surprised them when suddenly the wealthy boy and his father announced their thanks to the kennel boss and then exited the kennel without a word to them.

The mother stiffened at the offense. "What is going on?"

Without acknowledging her, the kennel boss swept the entire kennel floor with a short-whiskered broom while humming an ugly tune before ambling over to the main cage, unlocking it, and unceremoniously expelling their female man.

The boy took his female man into his arms. She was happy to be out of the cage and happy to be hugged.

The kennel boss said to the mother as she signed the release form in the designated places, "His boy says he is a friend of your boy, so no harm done. It was only a scratch anyway. But they do have a few demands. You will pay to have the latch on their door repaired, or they will have her thumbs removed. You will build her a proper kennel with a proper lock to keep her at home—a proper lock which they will inspect upon completion, or they will have her thumbs removed. Finally, you will surrender the baby man—or mans—as soon as it, or *they*, are born."

The boy, hugging his female man, glanced up and echoed, "Baby man?"

"What baby man?" the mother asked sharply.

The kennel boss had refilled his cup and now he took a long slurping sip from it, gurgled, and gave the stuff caught in his teeth another good suck through. "Your man is pregnant, in case you didn't notice. As I told you, they are only good for two things, hunting and giving birth. She has been sneaking out of your yard to take company with one of their mans. Now she is pregnant and her litter belongs to them," he proclaimed airily.

The mother seethed. "That is the very height of cruelty to mans! I will not sign to have her give up her child!"

"But you have already signed, Madam Pinhead Oaf!" taunted the kennel boss, snatching up the papers the mother had signed and waving them in her face.

When she lunged for them, he pushed them into a drawer, locked it, and coolly ordered her and the boy to take their man and leave.

3

A Proper Kennel

The sermon was about loving all creatures great and small, and the boy, who usually fidgeted in church, listened today with attentiveness to the sacred speaker's words. It seemed to the boy that the sacred speaker, who was also his history teacher at school, was addressing the message especially to him as they kept making eye contact.

"And now we come to the mans," spake the sacred speaker. "Of all great nature's creatures, he is the most like us in appearance and habit. There are those among us who say that the mans are related to us. In truth, they are like unto us in appearance. Their life span is but a third of ours, but the stages they go through are identical to those that we go through. Like us, they are hunters. Left on their own in the wilds, they dominate the other creatures, hunting and harvesting them as they see fit. They can use simple tools. They can build shelter, of a sort. Indeed, some among the educated say that mans are related to us. Some go so far as to speculate that we are descended from them. That they are an unevolved form of us. Or that from the mixing of their blood and angels', came we. I don't know anything about that. I know only that great scripture says that we have dominion over them as we have dominion over all beasts. This does not mean that we are to abuse and mistreat them. This means that we must be wise stewards of the land and all the creatures in it. We must not abuse them when they are our pets. We must not over-hunt them in the wild. We must see to it that their natural habitats in our forests and our swamps, in our seas and our mountains, in our deserts and our frozen places, are protected from overhunting and from the encroachment of our civilizations. The other day, I took my son on an adventure to the southernmost end of our continent, just before the place where the great sea abuts the sandy shore and to the west where flows the great river of grass. And we did walk in our water shoes to the very end of our civilization where the land becomes more water than soil. We were in the swamp of the crocodilians and the mans. We were in the swamp that is named the Eternal Grass. There were birds aplenty, amazing aviators and hunters these. Wading with legs like long reeds in deep water, these feathered fowl of the water and of the air hunted with long snakelike necks and sharp swordlike beaks the abundance of fish swimming in schools around their submerged feet. There were enormous turtles there with leathern shells and varicolored faces, sunning themselves on the rocks as they watched the hunting of the birds. There were creeping creatures, furry rodents scurrying up the trees and slithery snakes making their way through the grasses. There lurked by the hundreds the large somber scavengers in black, the hunchbacked and hooked-face vultures. And there were other birds, hundreds of other birds, flitting through the sunlit skies, loudly singing their various songs, their boisterous cacophony of joy—joy at being alive—alive, yes, alive and happy to be in that moment right then and there in that holy tabernacle of nature. In this wet place, in this place of water and soil and grass, life abounded in all its diversity. We watched from a safe distance and with respectful caution the lesser masters of the food chain of that region, the proud and awful crocodilians, the giant swamp lizards, the le-gators. Among all the creatures that walk on land or swim in sea, the le-gator possesses the most powerful bite. We were warned by the guide that the le-gator will eat anything that it can catch, including my son and myself if we were not careful. And while it looks slow and ungainly as it drags its large bulk out of the swamp to sun itself on the shore, we were cautioned that it has amazing and surprising speed, which was demonstrated when a le-gator, at rest on the shore, accelerated suddenly and caught and ate a large white-feathered bird which had been standing a seemingly safe dozen or so hla-cubits away. When the le-gator finished its feathern meal, it roared loudly, a roar that set all winged creatures to flight, and it slunk its bulk back into the water and swam out to the middle of the pond, its eyes and nostrils the only parts of its dragon-serpent body above the waterline. The guide explained to us that the le-gator, which was once hunted almost to extinction by our kind, is now plenteous again in the swamplands of the Eternal Grass after strict laws prevented hunting and poaching of the magnificent beast. The le-gator, as powerful and ferocious as it is, has but one enemy in nature, and that enemy is man. *But where is man, the greater master of the food chain?* my son and I wondered as we watched the great le-gator's leisurely swim. Then the guide cried, *Look over there!* as they burst through the trees—about a dozen of them—carrying long sticks sharpened on stone. These were not the mans that we have as pets. These were not the mans that we see in zoos or who perform for us at our circuses and festivals. These were feral mans—wild mans in their natural environment—with their lithe, naked little bodies covered over in dirt and mud. The stench of them reached foully across the pond to us, and we had to put our hands over our nostrils. They were the breed with lidless eyes and pale skin, though it was hard to judge the skin pigmentation with all of that dirt and filth on it. One of them had a length of braided twine, which he flung with perfect skill and aim around the neck of the great swimming le-gator that had just devoured the bird. As a team they hauled the le-gator up onto the shore—it took all of them pulling on the braided twine, for this le-gator was a monstrous creature that was easily the size of any three of them put together—and it fought against their makeshift rope, twisting and turning, whipping its great tail frantically, and snapping its mighty jaws dangerously. But there were no casualties of the swamp mans that day, as the nimble creatures danced out of the way of both whipping tail and snapping jaws. They stabbed him many times with the pointed sticks, and we watched in awe as the mighty le-gator began to weaken. Now the le-gator, in desperation, turned his face toward the swamp again, hoping to escape into the safety of the water. His legs clawed the muddy shore helplessly. The mans stabbed him a few times more with the sharpened sticks, and the le-gator with a final, loud roar yielded his life to death. Briefly did they look down upon his body with a kind of quiet reverence, and then they dragged it into the forest and were gone. Man is indeed dangerous in his beauty, invention, and skill. Among beasts, he sits at the top of the food chain. He is a top predator, as are we. But unlike us, man is not wasteful. He does not eat more than he needs. He does not hunt for sport or industry. He gives back to nature as much as he takes. He is at one with his environment."

The boy nodded his head. The sacred speaker seemed to nod back.

On his days off, the father would call the boy out to the backyard and they would work on the proper kennel that he was building for their female man. Until it was completed, she would, as required by the law, sleep in the house.

The proper kennel was three hla-cubits tall and four hla-cubits wide on each side. It would take up more than half of the backyard. Its walls were made of brass mesh and wood, its roof constructed of tin. When it was finished, it would have two windows of glass—one that looked beyond the yard, and one that faced the window of the boy's room.

The work was not difficult, but time-consuming and costly because of the legal constraints.

The father complained to the boy one day as they worked, "It would not be so bad if the authorities didn't come by every day to check on our progress. There is wood that is less expensive we could use. We could chop down a tree, but they won't let us. Chopping down trees is against the law. Trees are protected by the law! We must use these expensive, store-bought boards to build a house for a man—a pet! I guess that's just fine if you have the silver to throw away. And the roof does not have to be made of tin. We have old boards lying around the yard that would make a perfect roof, but it will not pass inspection. And the proper lock—where will we find the money to pay for a proper lock? And then turn around and pay for the lock on the door she broke on the home of the wealthy! Where are we going to find the money? Everything is about money. I am a loader, I make very little money. My pockets are not weighted down with silver, but here I am building this expensive house for a man! If she were not pregnant, I would kick her for the mess she has gotten us into. If she were not pregnant, I would beat her with a big stick. If she were not pregnant, I would put her to fight at the circus. If she were not pregnant, I would sell her as meat and pay for this expensive house I am building. And when the litter is born, can I sell it to make back some of my money? No. Instead I must surrender the litter to the wealthy! I could surely save a lot of money by just allowing them to remove her thumbs. I could surely save a lot of money by selling her for meat and then moving us all into this expensive house of hers that we are building. I would surely be better off if I lived as a pet. The government protects pets! What about protecting people?"

The boy, with tears in his eyes, passed the boards and the nails as his father labored and complained.

His female man, watching them, sat on the grass with her legs folded beneath her and drummed her thumbs on her expanding globe of a stomach.

The boy rubbed his eyes red and wondered at his female man drumming her pregnant stomach with her thumbs. Did she understand what his father was saying? That her thumbs would be removed to prevent her from breaking into houses and other mans' proper kennels?

He looked at her face, which appeared to have understanding. She seemed full of fear as she drummed her thumbs. She seemed full of fear and indecision.

"When I was a boy," spake the sacred speaker, "there were almost no mans left in the swamplands of the Eternal Grass because they had been hunted to near extinction. They were hunted for food, of course, and captured alive to be sold as pets, for they are easily domesticated and are loyal to their owners. I was told that back in those days, their number fell from several million to less than a few dozen in the swamplands. But stricter laws, which banned hunting out of season and which declared vast areas of the swamplands as a natural preserve for the mans, have brought their numbers back to a sustainable level. The last post–hunting season count put their number at close to half a million, which is a good thing for us, because without mans the swamplands were dying. The water was disappearing. The le-gator number was increasing, which meant the number of birds was decreasing, which meant the number of fish was increasing because there were no birds to feed on them, but they were sickly fish because the water was drying up. The swamplands smelled of death and decay. You see, man is not only a hunter that keeps the le-gator numbers in check, but a specialized herbivore that removes millions of pounds of deadly vines and weeds which clog the waterways of the swamplands. He feeds on these plants, which help in his digestion, and he also uses them to build the crude nest he calls a home. Man keeps the deadly weeds and choking vines in check. Man keeps the swamplands alive. Man is an essential part of the life system of the swamplands. Man brings life."

The boy bowed his head and made a reverent sound.

In the last week of the female man's pregnancy, the boy put on her leash and took her to the circus to see the fighting mans.

These were professional fighting mans, and the fights were exciting, with lots of punching and scratching and biting, as biting was legal in professional fights. His female man watched each fight with interest. At the end of each bout, the boy would point to the winning combatant and say to her, "Oh, he's not so tough. You could beat him, couldn't you?"

And she would nod her agreement and fire angry punches into the air, fighting an invisible opponent.

As they were leaving, they passed the stands where the singing mans were singing, and he felt a tug on her leash. He told her, "Okay," and she led him to the sound of music.

Onstage there was a man playing the singing harp, after that two female mans came on and played a colored flute and banged on a tinny drum, and finally three singing mans in blue appeared.

The boy and his female man leaned toward the stage to get a better look as the mans sang. Indeed, it was the three singing mans owned by the wealthy boy they had met at the field.

The one with the lidless eyes, the fattest of the trio, waved his fingers at the female man and she waved back.

As they sang, his female man shed tears and pouted.

When it was over, the boy went behind the stage to where the owners were leashing their mans after the performance.

The wealthy boy who owned the three singing mans in blue saw him and said, "They were good, weren't they?"

"They were very good," the boy answered.

"Has your father finished building the proper kennel yet?"

"Yes, she sleeps in it every night. She likes it a whole lot."

He did not tell the wealthy boy that because of the cost of building the proper kennel, their meals of late had been meager and many nights he had gone to bed with an anguished stomach that grumbled.

The wealthy boy was nibbling on a meat stick as he leashed his three singing mans. The poor boy watched the meat stick, his stomach grumbling. The wealthy boy caught him eyeing the meat stick, and the poor boy turned away.

The wealthy boy said, "Here, you can have one." He opened his sack and the poor boy saw inside, and there were meat sticks and candy rolls and sweet breads and every treat that a boy at a circus could ever want. The wealthy boy reached into the sack, withdrew a meat stick, and handed it over.

The poor boy thanked him and pushed the meat stick into his own empty sack and said, "I'll save it for later."

The wealthy boy passed him a sweet bread from the sack. "Friend, you're at the circus," he reasoned most kindly. "Eat something now."

The poor boy tore open the sweet bread and popped a piece of it into his mouth where its softness dissolved in a sugary deliciousness on his tongue.

As they ate their circus breads, the wealthy boy and the poor watched their mans.

The one with the lidless eyes was talking to the poor boy's female man. They listened as the man with the lidless eyes told her, "I will always be here. You never have to fear. I am your song bird forever and ever."

"The silly things mans say," said the wealthy boy.

"I once had a man that talked."

"Did you really?"

"I only had him for a week. He belonged to the mayor's wife. He was a runaway. I had to give him back. But then my father bought this one for me."

"She's beautiful," the wealthy boy said. "I like her hair cloths. Where did you get them?"

"My mother made them," the poor boy answered.

And they watched their mans and smiled with fascination when the one with the lidless eyes sang to the female man, "There is no reason to fear. I will always be here. I will always be here."

She made a cooing sound and touched his face with the back of her hand.

"There is no reason to fear," he sang, holding a high, beautiful note.

The wealthy boy said to the poor, "I think we're going to have to separate them before they go at it again and we get in trouble."

The poor boy agreed. "It's time for us to get home anyway. Thanks for the snacks."

The compassionate wealthy boy waved it off. "It's nothing. You want more?"

"If it's not too much trouble."

And the poor boy opened his sack, and the wealthy boy dumped all of the treats from his own sack into it. They shook hands as friends.

Then they created a secret handshake that only they two would share.

The poor boy said, "I'm sorry she bit you. She doesn't like strangers."

"It didn't hurt all that much. I'm sorry about what my father's doing to you and your man, and I hope we can always be friends."

"Friends forever and ever," the poor boy said.

And the poor boy and his female man left the circus grounds and went home.

"In the frozen regions of the north, we hunted the mans of the snow unto near extinction. Then we began to notice that the great white beos were vanishing too—and the great northern deer, and the great white wulf. The only creature on the increase was that pest, that vermin, the great white rat. It seems that the mans of the snow kept the great white beos in check. Left to their own devices, the great white beos overhunted the great northern deer—without the deer, the great white wulvs also began to decline in number, and then the beos too, as they were eating up their entire food supply, the deer! So, we emptied our zoos and reintroduced the mans of the snow to the icy frozen regions of the north. Twenty years later, their number is again close to what it once was, and not surprisingly the great white beo, the great northern deer, and the great white wulf have returned to plenteousness. The only creature whose number has declined is the pest, the great white rat. Great nature was set in motion by a lord wiser and mightier than we. He created nature and made of it a perfect balance. And in the frozen north, the mans of the snow are important to keeping the rigid line of balance on the scales of that life system. Without balance, there is death and decay. Remove mans and the ice melts into bloody water. A world without mans is a world without us all."

The boy nodded his head, silently mouthing the sacred speaker's words: *Perfect balance. A world without man . . . a world without us all.*

The baby man—there was only one—was born with much wailing and pain.

She was born at night—she was, like her mother, a female man—and the boy stayed by his window peering at the candle in the window of her proper kennel until the cries of a mother's agony were replaced by the sweeter cry of the newborn baby man.

As soon as he heard that, the boy ran outside and into the proper kennel where they all were gathered.

His mother was holding the baby female man in her arms and kissy-cooing her, and his smiling father was looking over his mother's shoulder and kissy-cooing too. His father hadn't mentioned anything about the cost of anything since she had gone into labor three and a half hours ago.

His father gushed, "She's beautiful. She's absolutely beautiful. The miracle of birth."

"She's beautiful like her mother, with red hair," the boy's mother said.

The boy pushed between them to see the tiny being in his mother's arms. He exclaimed, "She's got lidless eyes like the singing man and frecks all over her face like her mother!"

His female man made a weak plaintive sound in her throat and held out her arms, and the boy's mother placed the baby in her arms, and she held her child and kissed its face and nuzzled its wisps of bright red hair. She smiled warmly as she blessed the infant's pinkish face with kisses.

The boy and his family watched the female man and her child, and she fed her child, and a sweet sound came from its chest, and it rested its head on its mother's chest and went to sleep.

In the morning, before the sun rose, she came into the house and lifted the small singing harp from its pedestal. They followed her out to the proper kennel and looked on as she played the harp for the child. The harp sang a familiar lullaby: "Go to sleep, go to sleep, all is well, all will be well when you awaken, sweet one."

There were tears in the boy's mother's eyes, and his father held her. "Don't cry, sweet one. All is well," he told her. "All will be well."

She said through sighs, "I sewed some cloths for the baby's hair. For when she has more hair."

"Maybe they'll allow her to keep them," the father comforted.

"But will they allow her to keep the baby?" the mother sobbed.

The father breathed a gloomy sigh. "All will be well," he said.

It was early in the morning before the sun, and the father went to work, and then the mother, and the boy looked in on his female man and her baby man one more time and then latched the door of the proper kennel with its proper lock and went to school.

* * *

"In the western forests, we hunted the mans of the forest to near extinction. They were not the most appetizing, being lean and tough-muscled, but they made the best pets, for their nature was loyal and they had the gift of speech and mimicry. They could work in the mines. They could be bred with other man-forms to produce singing mans, and musical mans, and art mans, and thinker mans, and seer mans for the blind. But the tygas began to disappear. Then the olyphant. Then the red-breasted sparrow. Then the spiny roos. The green grass became black sand. And you may venture a guess as to how we solved the crisis in the western forests. We apologized to great nature for our error and returned things to the way they used to be. We had tampered selfishly without considering the consequences of our actions. We look at great nature and we see chaos and disorder. But seeing is a way of *not* seeing. We think that we can go in and straighten out the randomness and bring order. Build a dam here. Build a bridge there. Remove this life-form in large numbers here because it looks prettier over there. Seeing is a way of not seeing. It is a paradox, but true: the randomness and seeming chaos of great nature brings vibrant life in all its forms; the order and straightening out that our kind imposes on great nature brings death and decay. It is a paradox, indeed: order is death; disorder is life. We are cursed to have to learn this lesson again and again. In order to solve the crisis in the forests, we brought back the mans of the forest. The green of grass is the skin of the earth. Man scratches the skin when it itches. Soon the tygas were back and then the olyphants, the red-breasted sparrows, and the spiny roos. The despoiled grass grew green again.

The lesson here is take what you need from great nature, but don't overtake. And don't fix great nature—it isn't broken."

"It isn't broken," repeated the boy who owned the female man.

That evening as the boy, his mother, and his father were eating their dinner, there came a knock at the door.

The boy opened the door and there was his friend, the wealthy boy, but also his father.

There were other people with them, some of them looking important in uniforms or professional clothes. There were documents in their hands to be signed, and his father signed them wordlessly. His mother sat at the table, sighing with her head in her hands.

After the signing was done, one of the professionals who had come with the group asked, "Where is the infant man?"

The boy's father said, "She's in the back with her mother. There is a proper kennel in the back."

The professional asked, "Do we need light?"

The father shook his head. "No. There is light back there," he said, then led them through the grand room to the back of the house.

The wealthy boy walked side by side with the poor, upon whose shoulder his hand rested. "You can come over every day to see her. You can bring your man over every day to see her. So it will be like your new home, except that it's at my house. You can visit anytime you want, I promise."

Solemnly did the boys exchange their secret handshake.

When they got there, the door to her proper kennel would not open. The female man had propped something against it and they could hear the baby man crying inside.

The professionals looked in through the window and found her crouched down low. A plank of wood she had torn from an inside wall was angled against the door. Against this she pressed to keep them from entering.

One of the professionals nodded his head and another smiled. "Smart little female man," one said admiringly.

They leaned against the glass of the window, and when it broke, they reached inside and grabbed her. One of them strapped the muzzle over her face. The other picked up the baby and handed it to the wealthy boy's father.

His mother quietly wept, his father stood there with a hand over his mouth, and the boy restrained in his arms his muzzled female man, who clutched desperately for her child.

The boy shushed her and gently comforted, "It's going to be okay. I promise."

His mother quoted great scripture through her tears: "A mother gives life to her child. A mother gives her life for her child."

His father put his arms around his mother. "It'll be okay, beloved. I promise." He added gloomily, "She is but an animal."

His mother quoted scripture: "There is no sound in the world more sorrowful than a mother grieving her child."

When it was over, the boy stayed with his man in her proper kennel until she had ceased to weep. When she was finally asleep, he went back into the house and into his room where he sat by the window and stared out into the backyard. He fell asleep that night sitting up in bed by the window that looked out onto her proper kennel.

And the candle in the window of her proper kennel no longer burned.

Before the boy went to school the next morning, he brought out her food, but she was despondent and would not eat.

When he returned from school that afternoon and went straightway out to see her, she was asleep. He did not want to wake her, so he went back into the house.

As they ate their meal that evening, his mother said, "I think it is so cruel to take her baby like that. In my head, I keep hearing the baby crying. The cry is so sweet. It makes me so sad."

His father said, "Well, she's just an animal. She'll probably forget all about it in a day or two. They're not as attached to their children as we are."

His mother said, "The baby still cries in my head. I wish it would stop."

The boy jumped up from the table and ran out through the back door, shouting, "I hear the baby too, Mother, but not in my head!"

His father hollered after him, "Where are you going?"

They listened, but now there was silence in the back—there was not even the sound of the baby's crying in the mother's head.

The boy came back inside holding the baby.

His female man walked beside him.

His mother gasped.

The boy explained, "We should have fixed the glass window

in her proper kennel, Father. She broke out and went and got her. When I looked in on her after school she was sleeping, but I thought I heard a baby. She had hidden her behind her body to keep her from my sight."

His father said, "Well, now, this is bad. She broke out of her proper kennel and broke into their house again. This is very bad."

"They're coming again. You know that they are coming," said his mother frantically. "How much more of this can I take?"

"What are we going to do?" asked the boy.

"There's nothing we can do now but wait," said his father.

The female man had her hands out and the boy placed her baby gently into them. The baby made contented sounds as it received milk from its mother.

There was still food on the table, but nobody was eating as they watched the female man nurse her baby and then rock her to sleep.

There was still food on the table, and after a while the boy's mother got up and put everything away.

It was three days before they came.

This time they took both the infant *and* its mother.

When they brought her back late that night, her eyes were red from crying and both her hands were bandaged.

The professional who brought her back had papers for the father to sign and instructions on what was to happen next.

"You will be billed for the broken lock on the house she burgled. You will be billed for the medicals of those she bit. She bit the father, the mother, and their boy. They are nice people. They don't deserve this," he lectured. "And this is the bill for her medicals." He handed the father a folded card and a bottle. "This is the medication for her hands. Do not remove the bandages for two days. When you do remove them, rub this ointment generously on the place where her thumbs used to be. The doctor says that she should be back to normal in about a week. One thing is for sure—she won't be stealing other people's property anymore."

They all heard the sound and looked up. The weeping female man was in the grand room plucking the strings of the small singing harp, but without thumbs she could not make it sing properly.

The small singing harp sang, "Baabveee, baabveee, baabveee, baabveee."

It sounded vaguely like a song they knew. They could make out neither the tune nor the words, but it made them all very sad.

She never touched the small singing harp again after that night.

The wealthy boy continued to be the best friend of the poor boy, but his father would not let him keep his promise to have the female man come to visit and nurse her child.

He explained, "My father says that she is dangerous. It would be bad to have her around the baby man. She might try to harm it."

After that the female man became deeply dejected, though she lived another four months—one full man year—before the boy found her unmoving and unbreathing on her bedding in her proper kennel.

When they buried her in the backyard beside her proper kennel, the boy cried out, "Oh Red Sleeves, oh Red Sleeves."

The doctor said that she had died of a heart condition that was common among that breed.

But the boy believed, and always would, that she had died of a heart that was simply and irreparably broken.

"We are the rulers of this earth, which the lord great creator did give us to rule. On earth there is none greater than we. That which we envision we can build. That which we desire we can have. *All* that we desire we can have. But *should* we have it all since we can have it all? Should we take it all? And if we take it all, then what becomes of it? And after it is gone, and there is no more, what becomes of us? No creature on earth can say us nay. We as wise stewards of the earth are the only creatures that can say us nay. We must learn to say us nay," spake the sacred speaker.

And the boy lowered his head to hide the wetness in his eyes.

4
His Musical Man

After the female man died, the wealthy boy told the poor, "The baby man is yours. You can come to my house every day and watch them feed her."

And the poor boy did visit every day, for now he had no man of his own to love and his father possessed no discretionary money to purchase another.

At the wealthy boy's house, the poor boy was treated with a respectful sadness, even by the wealthy boy's father, who regretted originating the cruel though legal actions that had led to the unfortunate ending. Each time the poor boy visited, the father sent him home with a gift of food or silver for his parents, which the poor boy always accepted with discomfort and reluctance.

But the poor boy was not there for the generosity of the wealthy father nor even the friendship of the wealthy son. He was there for the infant baby man of his female man.

Each day she came to look more and more like her mother, with the red frecks on her face and arms growing rustier, and the red of her hair becoming more like fire.

The man's year is three times faster than the regular year, so at the end of the first year the poor boy had watched the baby man go from cradler to toddler and utter her first words. She was a man that talked, as had been her lidless-eyed father before her.

In the second year, the poor boy watched her grow from toddler into precocious childhood as she began early to display her natural gifts.

In his grand room, the wealthy boy's father had many instruments of music, enough for an entire orchestra, and the child man reached for the tinny drums and the colored flute and both the small and large singing harps, each of which she did play, for she was a musical man, as had been her mother before her.

The music she played was always bright and cheerful.

In her fourth year, when she was a budding prepubescent of twelve in man years, the child female man did become more melancholy, as did her music, as she went into heat and began to attract the attention of the man mans in the wealthy house.

The wealthy boy, who was twelve in regular years, did not want her to be fixed as his father had threatened. He told his friend, who was also twelve, "My father wants to have her fixed, but I have a plan. Why don't you take her? You still have the proper kennel your father built for her mother, don't you?"

The poor boy lit up. "That's a great idea!"

He exchanged the secret handshake with his friend and embraced him.

When the poor boy's father came home, he found his son pounding nails into the roof of the proper kennel in the backyard.

"I'm fixing it up. I'm getting a new female man," the boy explained.

His father's brows and spirit lifted. "The one with the red frecks? The one who is the daughter of your old female man?"

The hammering boy nodded.

He heard the muttered words beneath his father's breath: "It's a good idea, I suppose. But how are we going to pay for it?"

The boy stopped hammering nails. "It's not that much money—she's not a baby anymore and she's housebroken domesticated. It won't cost much. Anyway, there is the money I earn down at the mill."

The father nodded. *Down at the mill.* The boy worked with him as a loader for a few hours every day after school. The boy was a hard worker, not like some of the other goof-off boys who worked at the mill part-time. The father was proud of his son; every father should have a boy like him.

He said to him, "Very good, but if you ever run short, come to me. Together we will find a way."

The boy went back to pounding nails and the father leaned against the fence and said, "It is not true when your mother tells you that I do not like mans. I like them just fine, but when I was growing up, my mother and I lived on the edge of the wilderness in a dwelling on the farm of a friend of my dead father. Our living was hard because we had very little money. It was not a farm with animals, but with grain. I was a small boy and lonely because there was nothing to do and no one to play with. Yes, the farmer had two dogs, but they were work dogs and not very good for companionship. One day I went to the edge of the wilderness and I spotted a little man man in the long grass. He was feral, but I was a boy and lonely, so I coaxed him with a gentle voice and the few grains in my hand that were to be my lunch. Eventually he came out and took the grain. He was a short, round man with thick fingers, pale skin, and a bad smell. He was feral, to be sure, but he allowed me to pet him as he ate the grains. And I petted him until he finished the grains, and then he darted back into the long grass and disappeared from my sight."

As the boy labored and the father told his story, the father remembered their female man with a miserable sadness that the boy heard in his voice. The boy on the roof of the proper kennel looked down at the father. The father with the pain in his heart looked up at his boy. Father and son looked at each other, and the boy asked for a plank of wood. The father reached for one in the stack beside the proper kennel and passed it up to his boy, who returned to his mallet but did not resume his work. He listened to the father tell his story.

"The next day, I took my lunch to the long grass at the edge of the wilderness and my little friend appeared and ate the grains from my hand. I talked to him about whatever a boy of that age who is lonely talks about to a man and he seemed genuinely interested, for he remained quietly in place though he had finished eating and there were no more grains. So he was my friend and I went to visit with him every day. I grew very fond of him and I called him *Fat One.* One day when I got there, Fat One had brought with him another man. This man was taller than Fat One and with a fatter stomach, but with the same pale skin and a similar oval shaping of the eyes. I recoiled when I saw him, for his face made me wonder if he were dangerous. He had ugly bruises and gashes on his face as though he had been clawed by a predator or maybe even another man. I called him *Ugly One* and I fed him too, though I did not like him as much because of his damaged appearance and because he always rushed to grab the grains from my hand before I could give some to my little friend Fat One. One day when I went to the wilderness, Ugly One was there alone and he rushed to snatch the grains from my hand. Where was Fat One? Where was my little friend? While Ugly One ate his fill of the grains, I went into the edge of the wilderness searching for Fat One. I only had to walk a few hla-cubits before I found him lying on the ground, bleeding from a wound in his head. I was puzzled. What happened? Seconds later, my bewilderment was solved when Ugly One, having finished his meal, ran to Fat One and hit his head with a sizeable rock and began to dance and laugh. Like all boys, I had been warned never to trouble a feral man because they bite and they have diseases, but I became angry and I lifted Ugly One by the neck and slapped his face with my hand, crying, *Don't do that*! *Don't do that*! When I dropped him, he screeched miserably and ran off into the wilderness, never to be seen by my eyes again. Well, now I had to do something. I could not leave Fat One lying helpless on the wilderness floor. What if Ugly One returned to finish the job? What if some other predator found him? The truth was that I had been hoping ever since I'd found Fat One that my mother would allow me to keep him as a pet. So I picked him up and took him home, where I explained all that had happened to my mother. She nodded her head as I spoke, and then she took him from me, washed and scented him so that the bad smell went away, and then she laid out some sheets for bedding and placed him upon them. That night I slept on the bedding with my little man man Fat One beside me. In the morning when I awoke, he was doing much better and we played together all day. The friend of my father who owned the farm came to visit and he and my mother looked on as we played. And the friend of my dead father said, *The man cannot stay in the house. He will have to stay out in the yard.* My mother had a queer, sad look on her face, and she said to me somberly, *He will be safe in the yard.* Then she commanded me to take a nap and I did, and when I awoke from the nap, it was time for supper. I ran to the window to see my man in the yard, but could not. Well, it was a big yard. I would go out after supper and we would continue our play. So I ate my meat soup with grains that was set before me and thought nothing more of it. Afterward I ran back to the door, and my mother stopped me. *Where are you going*? she asked. *To play with my man*, said I. And my mother had tears in her eyes as she explained what had been done. The friend of my dead father had a great appetite for man, but they were scarce and dangerously feral in that part of the earth and thus expensively sold by the trappers and hunters. But a feral man made a pet of by a boy dwelling on his property? Indeed, it was his property, as was every beast living on it. He considered the gift of the quarter portion of Fat One that he had given us to make our soup quite a grand gesture on his part. My mother warned me that if I hoped to avoid sadness, I was never to bring home another man until our situation was improved or until the friend of my dead father had made of her a wife. The warning was unnecessary, for my stomach had already been forever turned."

The father, having finished his story, sighed and went into the house.

The boy, disturbed but undeterred by his father's story, hefted his mallet and resumed his hammering of nails.

When the boy arrived at his wealthy friend's house, only the wealthy father was at home and he bid him come in. They passed through the great house and to the back where the proper kennels were set up. Her kennel door was already open, and the boy reached inside and she came to him. She was pretty with her red hair in bright green hair cloths and her loins covered by a green pouch.

As he leashed her, he said, "You're going to live with me now."

She answered, "Yes, they told me."

The look on her face was not exactly joy, and he said to her, "You don't want to come live with me? You don't like me?"

"I like you very much. I guess it will be okay."

The boy glanced up at the wealthy father, who shrugged, and then he said to the little female man, "I thought you liked me."

"I like you just fine."

"But . . ."

"But *that place* is where my mother died."

"I liked your mother very much," he said.

"Yes, they told me. But you're very poor. Will I be able to eat every day?"

The poor boy flinched.

The wealthy boy's father smiled.

"Yes," the poor boy insisted, "we have food enough for you," though he knew there would not always be food enough for themselves. "You will eat every day. I am working at the mill to make sure that you are well fed. You will eat better than we do. Does that answer all your questions, little man?"

"Okay, I guess."

"What now?"

"Instruments."

"We have a small singing harp."

He saw the look on her face. *One* small singing harp?

He said, "It's the one your mother used to play . . . and I will work to purchase new instruments for you. In time you will come to own every instrument that exists. I promise."

It was a promise they all knew he could not keep, so the wealthy boy's father added, "And what he does not own, he is free to borrow from me."

She nodded at that, but the look on her face . . .

"What now?"

"Nothing."

"What? Tell me," the poor boy said.

The red-haired female man hid her face in her hands.

"What?" he said. "What?"

She blushed. "Well, it's just that I have someone here that I like. Will I be able to see him from time to time?"

"No!" said the boy.

The wealthy father shook his head. "No man mans for you. That's why we're sending you away. We're sending you away to keep you out of trouble. If we don't send you away, then we are going to have you fixed."

Now she was sobbing in big gulps. The poor boy rubbed her head and she peered at him through her tears. "What does that mean? Fixed? I'm not broken, am I?"

The wealthy father called the poor boy over and said to him, "I have some things for you. Some food for her. Some cloths for her hair. A few leashes. And some *things* for your parents."

The poor boy shook his head. "I'll take the things for her and the food for her, but not the silver. You have already given enough."

"The poor do not understand the heavy burden of silver," the wealthy boy's father said. "I am ashamed of what I put you through. You're a nice boy, my son's best friend, and your parents are good people. I was unkind and I acted selfishly. Please take this silver from me and give it to your parents."

And the poor boy took the silver for his parents.

When he got her home, his new female man seemed reluctant to go out to her proper kennel. Instead, she stayed in the house, exploring the rooms. When she finished exploring, she picked up the small singing harp and made it sing: "In the heart, in the air, hear the joy everywhere . . ."

The boy was amazed. "That song, your mother used to play that song."

"I know," she said.

"How do you know?"

"She told me."

"But how did she tell you? She's dead."

"Mother is she who gives all to her child. She's ever with me, telling me things."

At first, the boy believed her words and pondered their significance. Then it came to him that he was talking to a man. Sometimes they spoke sense, but more often than not they spoke nonsense that had the appearance of being sense. The boy knew that nothing that is dead can still be with us. But he smiled and decided to play along with her.

"What sort of things does she tell you?"

"She tells me that you are very nice and she loved you very much. You took very good care of her. You stood by her side in her trouble."

"Hmmm. Very nice. What else does she tell you?"

"That you are correct. She died of a great sadness in her heart."

The boy was no longer comfortable playing this game. He was starting to have a strange feeling. "How do you know that?" he demanded.

"She told me."

"But she is dead."

"She is with me now at this moment. I am filled with her."

He looked at her, and her green eyes had strangely darkened.

"She says that it was cruel of them to take her infant away. She was a mother, but not a mother. It was cruel of them to remove her thumbs. She had hands, but no hands. She could no longer make the small singing harp sing her heart's pain. She wept every night until the night she died."

"This is dreadful," said the boy.

"Truth is often dreadful," said his man.

The boy was weeping. "Does she tell you any *good* things?"

"She tells me good things, but those good things are for me alone, and not to be shared."

"Okay." He sniffed back tears.

"But she does not want you to weep."

"I can't help it. I miss her. I'm sorry how she died. I wish I could bring her back and save her life."

"Wait, I do have a good thing that I can tell you."

"Okay."

"She touched the heart of the father of the wealthy boy. He is afraid of me. He is afraid of you. That's why he insists that you take his silver."

"Really?"

"She commands him to do it. He is afraid that she will kill him. But she can't do that. She is dead. It doesn't work that way. There is no need to fear the dead."

"That's very funny," the boy said, and he laughed a small laugh.

She added, "I want those instruments in his house. I want *every* instrument in his house. He is afraid and he will give them to you if you are patient and ask for them one at a time."

"Okay," said the boy, laughing. "We will take all of his instruments. Hahaha. One at a time."

His female man laughed with him, and then she said, "I will tell you a good thing that my mother told for me alone and not to be shared. But she trusts you. I trust you. So I will share it with you."

"Okay."

"This world will die one day."

"What does that mean? Is that true?" He peered into her green eyes, which were now as dark as a forest blackened by fire.

"This world will die one day and all of this shall pass away. But I will not die here. I will die somewhere else."

"What does that mean?"

"I do not know," the female man said, "but it is what my mother told me and she does not lie."

And then she finished her song: "In the heart, in the air, hear the joy everywhere. Shall we call, shall we sing, of the joy everywhere? Come, my friends, let us sing, of the joy everywhere. There is joy, there is joy, there is joy everywhere."

And the day became evening, and his parents were at home, and they were happy to have a musical man in the house again. She made the harp sing for them as they ate their meal in happiness, and when evening became night, she slept under the boy's bed.

This went on for many weeks.

When the boy asked her if she wouldn't be more comfortable sleeping outside in her proper kennel, she told him, "I am afraid. Bad things happen to mans in proper kennels in this neighborhood. From what I see, some of them are desperate in this neighborhood. They are so poor and so hungry. To you I am a man, but what do you think I look like to them? Food. I could be stolen and eaten. You wouldn't want that, would you?"

"No," the boy told her. "That would be dreadful."

"Yes it would be," she said.

And they laughed together.

In four years, when the boy turned sixteen, his red-haired female man was eight in regular years but twenty-four in man years and in outward appearance. And in that year, the boy found a girl who was about his age and in the natural course of things he began to spend less time with his female man.

He would get up in the morning and feed her, then rush off to school, then after school he would work his hours at the mill, then he would come home and feed her, then don his finest garments and venture out with the girl with whom he was in love.

There were smiles all around the house, but there was a strain too.

One evening as he dressed, his twenty-four-year-old man said, "You know, I created a new song for you. Would you like to hear it?"

He said, "That sounds like a great idea. When I get back, you'll play it for me."

"Going out again?" said she.

"Yes, as a matter of fact, I am," said he.

He was prepared for a fight.

This time she surprised him by saying: "Have fun."

When he got back that night, he was too worn out, he told her, to listen to the song and he fell asleep right away. She played the new song to an audience of herself, then folded herself under his bed and went to sleep.

In the morning when they awoke, she asked him if he would like to hear the song she had created for him.

He said, "Sure. Play it."

She sat down with the small singing harp in her lap and began to make it sing, but there was a noise from beyond the room. Someone was at the door. When they opened the door, it was the girl with whom he was in love.

She said, "I came by to walk with you to school. Hey, that's a man! She's a cute one. Is that a singing instrument thing she's got? I always wanted a musical man, but, you know, my father could never afford one. All we ever had growing up were regular old run-of-the-mill mans. How did you guys get so wealthy?"

"We were blessed," the boy said. "She can talk too."

"Well," the girl said, "she must cost a lot. Tell her to say something. I love the way they talk. I see them all the time at the festival and the circus. Tell her to say something funny."

The boy looked down at his man, and she grumbled, "Okay, so now I'm a circus performer."

The girl looked at the boy, then back at the man, then back at the boy. "Is that it? Is that all she can say?"

"She can say more than that, can't you, girl?" he said, winking at his female man.

She scolded, "Hurry on your way to school, little children, before you are late."

The girl said, "That is soooooo cute! I love the way they talk. Can I bring my little brother over to play with her?"

The boy said, "Well, I'll have to ask my parents."

His female man quipped, "Well, maybe you should ask me. The answer is no. Goodbye now. Have fun at school, children."

The girl said, "That is soooooo cute! You are soooooo lucky to have her. She must be worth a lot of money."

The boy, sensing the shortening temper of his female man, who was known to bite on occasion, nudged his girl toward the door and they left for school.

His female man was named *Red Locks* because of the red hair on her head, but often the boy believed they should have named her *Red Mouth* because of the sassiness with which she sometimes spoke to him—and the painful man bites she sometimes gave him.

When the boy came home he fed his man, and the harp was in her hand as he dressed to go out again. He promised her, "Tonight when I come home, you can play the song you created for me as many times as you like. I will listen."

"Will you?"

"I promise."

"Will you?" said she who had been disappointed so many times before.

"I promise, I promise, I promise," said he who had disappointed.

"Okay, I'll try to wait up. If I'm asleep, wake me. An artist must have her sleep, you know?" She batted her eyes at him.

He petted her head. "You're still my favorite girl, okay?"

That made her happy and she waited up well into the night for him, but when the hours grew too long for her determined but limited constitution, she fell asleep.

She awoke with the next day's sun and pouted as he dressed for school. "You did not wake me last night as I told you to."

"I don't want to fight with you."

"Pinhead!" she called him.

"Who is the man and who is the master!" he fired back.

She shook her head from side to side and clucked her tongue with sadness as she set the small singing harp on her lap and played the song he hadn't asked her to play: "The way you treat me, the way you treat me, the way you treat me, my heart is unclear. The way you treat me, the way you treat me, the way you treat me, my heart is soooooo unclear."

At the completion of her song, he sat down on the ground beside her. "That is beautiful," he told her because he mistook the melancholy in the tune for cheer and he hadn't really been listening to the words. "You are the best musical man in the whole wide world."

She smirked.

"The *best*," he said with a wink.

She said, "I have to be honest with you. I don't like your girl and neither does Mother."

"Why not?"

"Mother says that she is no good for you."

"What makes her say that?"

"She is hungry. She thinks you can feed her."

"Oh, I see. But your mother is wrong this time. I am a poor boy. I can't feed anyone. She is with me because she loves me. She is beautiful. Don't you think she is beautiful?"

"This girl is beautiful like a poisonous flower. Her beauty is there to draw you to the poison."

He shook with laughter. "Oh, but wait. This is my man and my dead man talking to me. Hahaha. What a pinhead I am! For a moment there, I was almost listening to you. I have to go to school now. Goodbye and thanks for the lovely song."

He reached to pet her head and she grabbed his finger and bit it.

"Ouch!" he cried out. "Sneaky man!"

"Listen to me!" she screamed.

"You bit me! I should muzzle you!"

She put her hands on her hips. "You will do no such thing, you big oaf! How dare you threaten to put the muzzle on me. Ask her about her brother! Mother said to ask her about her bad little brother!"

Then, with violent possession of the small singing harp, she dove angrily under the bed.

And he kissed his finger where she had bitten it and left for school, an odd little smile on his face.

After school the boy went to the mill to work his hours.

After the mill he came home and ate a meal with his parents while his musical man played—the tinny drums this time. Over the years they had acquired most of the orchestral instruments in the wealthy boy's father's house because of his fear. But she had never played the drums at mealtime before.

She drummed to make you want to shake your hips.

His father looked up from his bowl. "She's drumming tonight. It's nice, though."

His mother said, "She's very talented."

The father said to the boy, who now wore no smile on his face, "You and your girl aren't going out tonight?"

The boy shook his head.

"What happened?" his mother asked.

The boy shook his head. "At school, we had . . . sort of a fight."

"Well, that happens. That's nothing to worry about. That's nothing at all," his mother said. "When your father and I were young—"

"Leave him be. Let him eat," said his father.

And his female man drummed to make you want to shake your hips.

In his bedroom that night, he told his man, "She says her brother, her little brother, has been recently released from incarceration. He is a thief. The authorities have him on their list. But that doesn't mean you are right. He may be bad, but she is my girl. She wouldn't do a thing like that to me."

"They are hungry in this neighborhood."

"But she loves me, I know it."

"She is hungry."

"No."

"The way she looked at me . . . she says I am worth a lot of money. You know if they sold me for meat how much they would get? You know if they sold me to a circus how much they would get? I play every instrument. I can talk. I should be owned by the wealthy who know how to protect their possessions. In this neighborhood, it is only a matter of time."

"So you want me to sell you to someone wealthy? For your safety?"

"No. I want to stay forever and ever with you. But you should never have brought her into our home."

"You're crazy."

"I'm crazy. I'm a crazy man."

"You're my favorite girl," said he to her.

"You're not so bad for an oaf," said she to him.

She laughed and went under the bed. He laughed and went to bed. He lay in his bed for many minutes, laughing, laughing, laughing, and *thinking*.

His laughter died away, and he took in a deep breath and then let it out. He got up and looked under his bed, where she awaited.

And her lips met his.

"Oh," he said, his heart filling with confusion.

He went back up to his bed. She was under his bed. Beneath him. His pet. His favorite girl.

Evening turned to night and night turned to morning.

For the boy, it was a morning that followed a sleepless night—a night of waking dreams.

In the morning he prepared her favorite meal in her favorite bowl and brought it to her, and she played him a sweet tune on the colored flute, a tune that made him feel as sweet as bright pink melting into light blue.

"Does it please you?"

"It pleases me," he said.

She did not speak of the kiss, he did not speak of the kiss, but he left for school and he thought of it and nothing else all day.

After school he worked his part-time hours at the mill.

When he got home, the authorities were there.

His mother was weeping. His father was angrier than the boy had ever seen him before. The house was turned upside down. Everything was out of place. All of the larger musical instruments were missing. Most of the smaller musical instruments were damaged, and the small singing harp was completely destroyed.

"What happened?" the boy asked.

"Someone burgled us and stole our man," his father said.

"I know who did it! If we hurry, we can get her back!"

The authorities gathered around as the boy told them about the girl with whom he was in love and her brother who had recently been released from incarceration.

The brother denied it, of course, but they traced the missing instruments of music to the hot shops, and the clerks at several of them identified the brother as the one who had sold to them, earlier that day, this instrument or that.

But the penalty for theft of a man was more severe than the penalty for theft of any other property, so the little brother of the girl the boy loved continued to deny having stolen the female man.

"I'm really sorry about what I did—but I didn't steal any man from your house. Maybe she snuck out and ran away. I remember leaving the door open. Don't they run away all the time? Well, that's what I heard anyway."

They knew that he was lying, but he refused to admit the crime.

He shrugged. "In a world without thieves, the wealthy become gods," he said.

They checked all of the local public kennels, and no one would admit to having purchased a red-haired female man from the brother of the girl with whom the boy was in love.

When the boy got permission from the authorities to check the inventory of all the local public kennels, he did so, but his female man was nowhere to be found.

A sympathetic kennel boss took the boy aside. "You have to understand how it is, son. I see that look on your face and I can only imagine the pain you're feeling right now, but what I'm going to tell you is as true as the day is long. She is in one of two places. She is in the mines or she is with a circus. These days, most missing mans are never recovered. It's not like before when there were ample mans to go around. A man would run away and someone would find it and bring it home or bring it here. My shop used to be stocked with as many talking mans as dumb ones. But with all of these new laws protecting the natural habitats of the mans and no laws protecting the natural rights of working people to earn a living in the mines, every talking man is worth its weight in silver. Cheap labor is the law of the land. Whoever stole your talking man got rid of her immediately—and a musical man too! Circus or the mines, and I'm betting the mines. Only the wealthy are still using them as pets. People are too hungry these days. I do not have one single talking man in my shop right now. I take in maybe three a week and they are gone within minutes. Your man would have to be pretty dumb and pretty dull to be a pet, but the smart ones—straight to the mines. Thieves know this. Business is good for thieves these days. A curse on all thieves!"

The boy went home with the horrible vision in his head of his sweet, sarcastic little red-haired female man working in the mines. He wept all the way home. He wept all night.

"Oh Red Locks, oh my little Red Locks!" he cried in his room that night.

In the morning he got up and dressed for school and then he left. After school he went to the mill and he worked his part-time hours. After work he and his father got with their mallets and other tools and they tore down the proper kennel in their backyard.

It was a very long time before the boy courted a girl again. It was a very long time before he loved a girl again. And he never again owned a man.

It hurt too much.

5

Red Man, Red Man, Why Do You Weep?

War is king of your philosophies. Your harvest of blood fills your belly while infants and orphans wail.

—Great Scripture

On the day the red-haired female man arrived at the mines, the boss took the measure of her and liked what he saw.

He would have preferred that she not be so pale. On the other hand, two years in the eastern mines had made her lean, strong, and clever. He put her to work on the load-and-pull and found that she could do it better than any other man, and so he put her to lead it.

They told him she was a vicious fighter, that she had the gift of landing the first blow. The winding scar on her arm, they told him, was proof. He checked the scar and decided he may have been deceived. It may have been got from the lash. She was a talking man, and so he asked her.

"I have been defeated," she said. "But never by the same man twice."

Feisty, he thought, and he patted her head, his lips curling upward in delight. "I shall call you *Red Man*, for you have red hair."

She winced and he took notice. Fearing a man bite, he withdrew his hand.

The boss was first among poets.

How serious are her eyes, he thought. They are alert and at the same time so weary.

He peered into her emerald eyes and was afforded a hint of what two years of working in the eastern mines could do to a man—two regular years (six man years) of breaking rock and stone with hammer and club, of hauling the overloaded wheeled carts, of hefting granite, coal, slate, and silver, in the dark bowels of the earth.

"But," he said to himself, feeling a sudden surge of compassion, "here in the western mines, it shall not be so."

As soon as he said it, he took it back: "On the other hand, there is much silver to be made." He rationalized, "She is but a man, after all."

The boss was first among gamblers. He made her his favorite so that in lean times she would not be eaten as others had been. He made her his companion in the planning of strategy against the man who would be sent to meet her in the fight yard behind the food wagon.

He would point to the opponent. "Gold Braid does not weigh so very much, but she is tall with sharp teeth."

His female man would nod. "I will run against her and knock her to the ground. Then I will pounce quickly and pin her arms. I will twist like so to avoid her teeth, and I will bite with mine. Mine are sharp too, you know?"

"Good plan, my little red top," he would say, and then he would clap his hands. "See to it then!"

That is the way it went in the western mines.

She lived for the day's labor.

She lived for the day's opponent.

He was called *Yellow Fellow*, for his hair and his flesh were yellow-hued, and he was the champion.

Like her, he was a talking man. Like her, he was a man of talent, and his talent was word singing. The boss would watch the mans as they gathered by the fires to listen to the word songs of Yellow Fellow, and he would send Red Man to join him as companion in music. She played on a kind of tinny drum she fashioned out of whispering stones and coal rocks of differing size.

The word songs of Yellow Fellow were very beautiful, and every man listened with attention unflagging.

Even the oafs would gather behind them and hum the parts they knew. But when the food wagon was delayed, the hungry ones entered the tents of mans with their long knives and pick-sticks drawn. The chant of *Pick one, pick one, pick a nice fat one* rang out through the death-still air of the black night, and every man cried out to the great creator for deliverance.

"Let it not be me! Let it not be me!"

The red-haired female man cried out for all mans: "Surely, you cannot eat us! We are your mans! We work by your side in the mines!"

The oafs would have eaten her to silence her cries, which troubled their sleep as well as their minds, but she was spared, for she was a favorite of the boss of the mines.

When they complained to him, he sucked his teeth. "Leave her be. It is but the cry of a man. Sleep through it."

When she entered his tent and blasted her complaints loudly against his ear, he came to understand what the others meant when they said it was a disturbance to their sleep.

He put the muzzle on her and rolled over with his back to her. It helped but a little. She was his favorite, but as he lay there, a common working oaf, his precious sleep disturbed by the yapping of a man, he hatched a plan to punish her that brought a smile to his lips, if not relief to his ears.

The plan had much to do with her companion in music, Yellow Fellow.

He had a stout belly and was larger than she was—and he was stronger too, they knew, from his feats in the mines.

One day the boss watched amazed as Yellow Fellow saved her from a heavy stone that was falling, catching it with one hand and shoving her to safety with the other.

But outside the mines, he was sluggish and not much interested in the matches, most of which he won by intimidation into submission with his greater size.

He was not swift. He was not graceful. He quite often stumbled and bumbled into victories. No, he was not a great champion. He was champion by default, and he was the favorite of a lackadaisical and overconfident oaf who needed badly to be relieved of his silver.

"You are quicker than he is, true. But how will you turn advantage to victory?"

"His real weakness is his thin legs. I will knock against them, and when he topples I will wrap my arms around his neck. And then his battle is lost. I may not even have to apply my teeth."

The boss nodded. "Good plan, little red top. Although," he suggested, "I think you should apply your teeth regardless."

She peered back with eyes that were dangerously weary, as though she wanted to apply her teeth to *him*.

"But I guess that is your choice to make." He sucked in his cheeks and stepped back. "See to it then!"

They faced off behind the food wagon, everyone in attendance anticipating a great battle. But Yellow Fellow was too slow, too sluggish that day; she fearless and quick. In a flurry of noise and dust, it was over.

To all watching, the battle was hard fought and hard won, though brief. To the boss's thinking it could have been harder and longer, but he happily collected his winnings from the gamblers who had wagered on the wrong side. With a wide grin, he relieved Yellow Fellow's oaf of his burden of coin.

Then, since his pockets were heavy with silver, he extended the respite between periods of labor and demanded of the musical man a song. Yellow Fellow arose and cleared his throat. Red Man got with her whispering stones and her coal rocks of differing size to join him as companion in music.

And Yellow Fellow was a great singer of word songs.

He sang the Word Song of Elber-So-Wadle and the Village of Mans. And the bard did sing:

In days of old, Elber-So-Wadle was betrayed and banished into the wilderness by the treacherous Ti-So-Wadle.

In the wilderness, the great lord Elber-So-Wadle did wander forty days without food and finally did collapse on the ground.

On the ground did he collapse.

He awoke in a bed too short for his legs.

When up-he-got to investigate, his head he-did-bump on a ceiling too low.

He bumped his head on a ceiling too low.

The room was furnished so small he thought he had been made to rest in the room of a child.

Then down-he-bent so as not his head-to-bump upon entering the grand room of the house.

He saw therein a couch, two chairs, and a hearth, again befitting a small child.

Elber-So-Wadle scratched his head in wonder.

"Perhaps I am still dreaming," to himself said he.

"Still dreaming am I perhaps," he said.

Then down-he-bent and out-he-went and found himself in surroundings familiar:

Trees, bush, farmyard, barn;

Hoss, bovin, chicken, little chickees.

But the farmer, his wife, and their children were all mans!

Farmer, wife, children were mans!

The great warrior Elber-So-Wadle did near faint at the sight.

The man man farmer said to him, "Ti-So-Wadle has betrayed you and wishes you dead;

"But this is your rescue from the great creator who knows that you are just and good;

"And you shall lead his people in right-eous-ness.

"In righteousness shall you lead them."

"But who are you?" the great Elber-So-Wadle asked.

"I am Zack, the man man farmer, and this is the Vill-age of Mans."

"Welcome, great lord Elber-So-Wadle, to the Vill-age of Mans!"

"The Vill-age of Mans welcomes you!"

And here the bard did end his song.

The applause was great from both oaf and man. In admiration, the female man touched the man man's cheek lightly. Then the companions in music, Yellow Fellow and Red Man, bowed and said their final goodbyes.

When the bell tolled the end of respite, all went back to the mines and resumed their labor.

At the end of day when they bore him away, she followed as far as they would allow. From the basket where he awaited his fate, Yellow Fellow saw her and the boss heard him say: "I thank you."

"For what?" she asked.

"For the gift of song."

"Oh, that." She looked around first, searching for those who might overhear. Then she whispered, "And I thank you for my victory, sweet one."

Just as I thought, said the boss, who had often observed their sneaking off together.

He ordered her to leave, and she tightened her face to hold back the tears and she left.

Now we shall see, the boss said.

When they were finished with him, the boss hid some scraps of man flesh in the flesh of a bovin, and bid her come eat. She preferred, as did most mans who were not feral, a diet of vegetables and grain. In the mines, however, mans were made to eat whatever was put before them, despite their stomach's revulsion to it.

She took a bite of what she believed was a slice of bovin, but her stomach reacted to it with a different type of revulsion. She said to the boss: "It does not taste the same as it did before."

He burst into laughter. The female man lifted her eyes from her bowl and spied atop the table of the oafs, the well-cooked arms and legs of her great opponent. Her stomach heaved and surrendered all that was in it.

The boss and his companions around the table shook with laughter at the new champion chucking up the flesh of the old.

The boss was first among poets and he led them in song: "Great lord Red Man, oh mighty Red Man."

The others chanted, "Wel-come to the Village of the Oafs! The Vill-age of Oafs welcomes you!"

And the bard did sing: "Out here in this blackness, this loneliness, this place of barrenness, horror, and stone, the bitter tears of Red Man began to flow."

Someone touched her shoulder. It was her companion in music, Yellow Fellow!

They embraced, and the boss heard the man man say: "It was a joke they played on you, sweet one. Wipe your tears away. Oh, but I'm glad to be alive."

"You're glad to be alive?" The female man did not wipe her tears away, but continued to weep.

The boss came to her and petted her head. "Red Man, Red Man, why do you weep? It was only done in fun."

She winced at his touch and he pulled his hand away, fearing her teeth which were bared.

"He is just glad to be alive," she said, pointing sadly to the table, "but there is still a well-cooked man on your plate. Why can Yellow Fellow not understand this? How can he be so selfish?"

Her tears continued to flow.

"Out here in this blackness, this loneliness, this place of barrenness, *selfishness,* and stone, the bitter tears of Red Man continued to flow."

And here the bard did end his song.

6

The Bridge

The sun still rested in its dark bed when the boss was awoken by a jangling as of much metal. He quickly opened his eyes, for he thought someone might be troubling his silver. At the entrance to his tent stood a wide oaf in a scarlet tunic of brass.

He announced, "Today, you shall not go to the mines, but to war."

"Huh?"

The boss still had much sleep in his eyes. He wanted to roll over on his cot, but in the face of this visitor with the sword at his side there was only seriousness. The boss, accustomed to being the one who barked the orders, was reminded of his manners.

"What am I to do?" he implored with all due politeness.

"Gather your oafs *and* your mans," the soldier said, and then he explained to him what and why.

Afterward the boss ran into the tent of his red-haired female man and shook her awake. She looked around. "It is still dark."

"Early-morning darkness is the best time for war, it seems."

She rubbed the sleep from her eyes. "What is war?"

"War is like a battle in the fight yard, a battle with all of your companions against all of the other's companions, but with blades that chop and much more blood."

She nodded as though she had understanding. "And we chop them in order to gain collective victory. I have heard many oafs talk of this war thing," she said. "But don't people fall in war?"

"Yes. Yes," he said, and he thought, *Oh great creator! but she is a clever little man.*

He continued: "And if your companion is to fall, then you are to chop whoever did fell him. In other words, if I am to fall, you must set upon whoever felled me, you understand?"

She said, "Oh, so now I am your companion?"

"Yes!" he insisted. "Are we not companions?"

She hesitated. "I guess."

The memory of the trick played on her with Yellow Fellow was still fresh in her mind. The look on her face asked a question.

"What is it, little man?"

"When you fall, what am I to do then?"

He corrected, "*If* I fall, and hopefully that will not happen, but if it does . . . well, I guess you are to join with other mans whose oafs have fallen and set upon whoever it is that is setting upon them."

She frowned. "All this setting upon and setting upon, what does it really mean?"

He bumbled through poetic, grandiloquent, rambling answers that he could see from her expression she found less than convincing, but as he talked the confusion on her face disappeared and a kind of respectful boredom settled in.

Obediently, she went into each tent of mans, roused them, and they all came out, whereupon they lined up in order to be told what the oafs required of them so early in the morning.

Was the food wagon again to be delayed? Were they all to be eaten? What a grand meal that would be, for every tent had been emptied and every man assembled.

And is that snow on the ground? But it is not even the season. Wait! That's not snow, though it shines as white. It is the gleam of blades reflecting the light of the moon, blades so unlike the dull gray tools used in the mines. Blades for labor, no doubt. But labor of what kind?

And just what is this thing called *war* that Red Man told us about when she roused us from our needful slumber?

They waited quietly as they had been trained by the cudgel and the lash to do.

"War," said the wide oaf in the jangling tunic, "is where you're going today, because the army said why not use talking mans as soldiers? Why not use them to fill the gaps where soldiers who are dead used to be? They can take orders. They can hold a sword."

That made sense to the boss, and he nudged his female man, who was standing at his elbow. "Isn't that true?"

"Yes. We can certainly take orders," she said.

It took a few minutes of blows to the head and kicks to the gut, but the wide oaf finally taught them to stand at attention. Other oafs passed through the columns of mans and draped over each small body a tunic of brass, which clattered and tinkled musically when the man moved about in it. There was wonder in the eyes of the mans as they looked at the symbol on the breastplate.

The boss draped a tunic over his female man, and she said, "What is this black star?"

The boss silenced her with a finger. "Shhh. Listen to him."

"That," the wide oaf announced to all, "is your standard. Your standard is how you know what side you're on. In war, you can't go in there and chop just *anybody*. The goal of war is to go in there and chop anybody not wearing your standard. Now look at that standard. Anybody not wearing that standard, you chop him, and be he oaf or be he man, you chop him good."

Each man looked at the standard. It was a black eight-pointed star on a scarlet background.

The boss looked down at his female man, and she said, "I like the part about chopping oafs, boss. Don't you?"

He smiled back uncertainly. The usual weariness in her eyes was replaced by a twinkle that could be taken for playfulness, or malice. He could not decide which.

Another oaf said to the wide one, "It's time."

The wide oaf commanded, "Hurry now! Grab a sword as you pass. Chop anybody not wearing your standard. The enemy is poor, he is savage, and he is polluting the earth with his foul presence. They want what we've got, and we're not going to give it to them, and that's why we must win this war. Nobody wants to live in a world where the poor don't know their place. All praise be to the great leader! Now bow your heads!"

The oafs bowed their heads.

"Oh great creator, protect us as we do your will. And if we fall in battle, remember us evermore in your kingdom to come!"

"Verily in your name!" the others said as one.

"Verily in your name!" the wide oaf said. "Now move out! Fight for freedom! Fight for your side!"

The boss was first among poets, and he whispered to his female man: "A slayer of the innocent and the merciful of heart, is war. Stay close to me and you shall live. Ah, war. When this is over, there are more battles to be won in the fight yard. There is more silver to be taken from the careless and the unwary."

Then the mighty host of mans and oafs hoisted the standard of the black eight-pointed star and lumbered off to war, their scarlet tunics of brass singing.

And the female man came to know what war was, if war was shivering in the cold dark morning as she followed the standard for two hours up a steep mountain trail.

If war was metal projectiles pinging and popping all around her like angry applause.

If war was fire sprouting like bright red flowers too hot for fingers to pick.

They came to a broad, wooden bridge and made it halfway across. Over the noise of battle, there rose the pounding of drums, the pealing of trumpets, and a battle cry like a great screeching fowl, as tunics of black swarmed down the mountain. The enemy!

War had become bursting shells, foul smells, and bodies pressing against bodies, each side thrusting with sword and bullying with battle axe to establish a position of dominance on the bridge. The bodies were packed in tight and were heavy. The bridge, weighted to its limit, swayed. They pressed against each other, metal clanging against metal, each side pushing forward with javelin, battle hammer, pick-stick, and bludgeon to drive the other back or knock the other off the bridge.

As the bridge swayed, the female man's side was pushed back and back and back. She struggled to hold her position as well as keep her balance. The strain was too much. Twisted slantwise, she was still falling. She would tumble into the murky water. And her side was still being pushed back. Back.

Just as she felt herself going over the edge, her feet met solid ground again. But it was muddy ground, and slippery. She swung her blade and lost her footing. The blade was whacked from her hand. She reached down to retrieve it and could not believe her eyes. Where was the earth? Where was the earth? The fertile earth had been turned to crimson mud.

"Oh lord great creator, not this!" she wailed.

To her right, the female man Gold Braid was felled by an arrow. To her left, the musical man Yellow Fellow was trampled underfoot by sandals of brass. Ahead of her, the wide oaf stepped into a nest of bursting shells and was set ablaze. As all around her oafs and mans fell, she took a blow and went down.

But the boss was first among gamblers, and he raised his sword. "After war there is much silver! Rise up! Strive on!"

The female man climbed back to her feet.

The boss clanked his sword on his shield proudly. "That's how it is with war, my little red top! The battle is not to those who fall last, but to those who rise back up first."

Then he felt a sudden pain as his belly was torn by a blade thrust into it. He shouted a profane oath and cried: "Undone—and on the first day of battle!"

His belly was split in two. All that had been in it was coming out. Ideas rampaging through his brain, he struggled to come up with an adage to sum up the strange quality of his situation, but he found it difficult to organize his thoughts. A *battle raging in the belly is war? War is a belly split in twain? War is a belly with its silver spilling out?*

When he went down, he scowled as the enemy who had felled him extended a hand to his little female man. He grimaced as she grabbed back. He shouted, "No, little man! That's not how it's done!"

He looked on helplessly as the enemy lifted her, kissed her cheek, and carried her back across the bridge, sheltered within his brass tunic of war. The boss did not know what to make of the scene. It was difficult to think with his stomach on the ground beside him. The words to describe it he struggled to find. Just before he died they came to his lips: "Compassion for one's enemy is a most rare and beautiful thing."

And the poet closed his eyes.

Almost as soon as he had closed them, he revised the adage: "Compassion for one's enemy is rare, beautiful, and *almost* as wondrous as a belly full of silver."

And the gambler opened his eyes nevermore.

7

Man at War

She knew caves, so she knew that she was in a cave, a cave lit by waxen candles, and gathered around a table studying a map were the leaders of the oafs with the tunics of a different standard.

And the different standard was a scarlet eight-pointed star on black.

In the cave there were other oafs. Many of them had deep cuts and frightful scars. All of them had swords. Many of them lay on cots. Those who had not cots were seated on the ground on rocks, and they leaned against their swords. Their eyes were closed. They were resting while waiting for the war to continue.

On the floor of the cave were the bones of mans. The bones were picked clean.

There was a fire and a spit.

There was a man roasting on the spit while an injured oaf slowly turned him by winding the handle. The man was charred already. One of his charred legs was missing. The injured oaf slowly turning the spit was nibbling on a charred leg of man. He sniffed the man on the spit to see if he was done being cooked. From her years in the mines, she knew the smell of well-cooked man. The smell turned her stomach. This man on the spit was well cooked.

The oaf turning the spit saw the red-haired female man looking and leered at her with an open mouth that was missing all but three of its teeth. "The red-haired one awakens."

The others looked at her with bored indifference and went back to resting on their cots or against their swords, or studying the map.

Now she knew another quality of war. War was when oafs were so tired from fighting each other that they would rather rest against their swords than torment you.

She was in a cave of the east, where she had toiled for two years, and she ate from the bowl of grains they had set out for her and drank from the bowl of water beside it. She must be a favorite again, she thought.

The other mans in the cave were each bound together or caged together or roasting on the spit or littering the ground as bones and blood.

But she was left unbound, uncaged, and uneaten. Where was the boy of her childhood who had rescued her from the battlefield? Where was he?

She slept and then she awoke and then she slept again. When she awoke the second time she observed that the cave was being used as a place to care for the sick and as a place to plan the battles. All day long new oafs with new injuries came and were tended to and then went back to the war. Some came to eat from whatever meat the three-toothed oaf was roasting on the spit. Some came to rest. Some came to lay their bodies down and die. At the end of the day, the first boy of her childhood, the boy of the wealthy, came, laid his body down, and died.

They stacked him on a heap of bodies that was piling ever higher. When the heap was piled high enough, they pushed it out of the cave in barrows and set it on fire. She was careful to conceal her tears from the oafs, but they did fall.

Some came to gather around the table with the others looking at the map. She heard one of those looking at the map say, "It is going well. It is going as well as could be expected. In a few more days it will all be over."

Another map reader said, "Yes, everyone did a great job. Many are to be congratulated. It shouldn't be much longer before we take the mines."

"It is a great day, Gen'rl," said the first.

"After we take the mines, we will have the advantage. There is no going back now."

"We shall raise our standard and be proud."

"We shall overrun their cities and make our demands. There shall be blood in the streets. The people shall rule the day. The wealthy shall be taught a grave lesson."

"Blood will settle these warring philosophies."

"War is the king of philosophies."

"It is a great day."

The oaf called Gen'rl yawned. "Now I can rest, as I have done my duty to the best of my abilities. I have served the people. I can rest now, because we have all of us done a great job. It is a great day.

I am going to rest on my cot and no one is to awaken me unless there is very good reason. And when I awaken I will eat. Prepare one of the mans for my meal. That one there will do, the one with the red hair."

She gasped as the oaf called Gen'rl pointed to her.

"But she is a favorite of Luf'tnt Auutet, sir," spoke a subordinate officer of the oafs, out of turn, to the one called Gen'rl, who responded to him with a look in his eyes like a great burning fire.

The subordinate officer bowed and uttered an obsequious apology and then quickly gestured a command to the three-toothed one that roasted mans slowly on the spit.

Obediently the three-toothed one hefted a large stone club in one hand, lumbered over, and grabbed her by the neck.

Swinging her arms and kicking with her legs, she struggled to free herself from the oaf, but she was grabbed and grabbed well.

The cave stank of death and other filths, as these were the unclean oafs. The cave, though it was a place of healing, was littered with their waste and the discarded remains of the mans they had eaten.

The one called Gen'rl stretched himself out on his cot. His subordinate officer, who had spoken out of turn, removed a small singing harp from his sack and set it on the table with the map, which was now rolled into a tube.

The subordinate leaned back against the table and ran his fingers over the strings. The small singing harp sang: "Justice vision, Justice true, fair to the unfair, Justice bleed, Justice be, fairness and equality, Justice be . . ."

As the music played, the oaf with three teeth in his mouth swung the female man down to the ground when he found a good clean flat place upon which to bash her brains out. She landed on her back. He pressed her down with one hand as he raised the club. But she arched up, flipped away, landed on her feet.

Ran.

He came after her swinging the heavy stone club, which quaked the earth each time it landed.

"Get away from me!" she screamed as she ran.

The others, laughing and calling, "Pick one, pick one, pick a nice fat talking one," rose up, as did their spirits, and joined in the chase.

She was limber and swift, and she eluded them as she ran to the mouth of the cave.

Laughing and calling and making jokes at each other's clumsiness, they reached for her and missed, and laughed some more. The one with the club swung it down, quaking the earth beneath her feet. "Fi! Fi! Fi!" he laughed.

She ran. She was almost at the entrance to the cave, but the one who had lost an eye got up from his cot, his mouth a gaping black maw of hawing laughter, and he jumped in front of the entrance, blocking it. He crouched low with his hands out to catch her.

She stopped in midstride and abruptly changed direction. Now she was running toward the one with the small singing harp.

He saw her coming, set it down on the table, crouched low with his arms outstretched and his mouth open in hawing laughter. He waited to catch her.

Narrowly escaping his grasp, she changed her direction again and went up this time.

Up!

Now she was leaping up to the top of the low table, and as they grabbed and clutched after her, she reached for the small singing harp.

She felt them grab her, and grab her well, and lift her. She felt their stinking laughing breath in her hair. She felt the small singing harp in her hands. She felt the familiar strings against her fingers. She felt their teeth in her hair. She closed her eyes and rubbed the strings.

The small singing harp sang: "Justice vision, Justice true, fair to the unfair, Justice bleed, Justice be, fairness and equality, Justice be. Justice we, Justice share, Justice to the unjust, Justice share. Justice of my father, Justice of my land, Justice of the people, Justice be . . ."

They had set her down on the table. They were singing along in somber voices. Some were saluting. Some were shedding tears.

One was wailing mournfully, "Fi, fi, fi. Ooohhh, fi, fi, fi. Must war always be the oaf's schoolmaster? So many comrades have fallen beside me in battle. So many noble oafs I have slain. The sun rises in gold and sets in blood. Let it be worth it, oh lord great creator. Oh, let it be worth it."

One of them said, "She's one of us. She plays the anthem. She was a spy for us in their tunic."

"She may be a spy for them. How do we know she's not spying for them?" said another.

"Because she's playing our anthem, pinhead!" the first one growled, spitting.

"Who are you calling pinhead?" the second one said, his hand dropping dangerously to the handle of his blade.

Before it could come to blows, the oaf called Gen'rl arose from his cot. The soldiers parted down the middle to make a path for him to the table. His brow knit up in oafish thought, he peered down at the red-haired female man in the tunic of the wrong standard and with the small singing harp singing in her lap. He was silent for many moments before he spoke to them with the authority of his rank.

"She's a man. Mans don't spy. They're putting these little mud mice in the war but they call us savages because we eat them. Oh, fi, fi, fi. They ran is what they did, all of them, dropped their little blades and ran. They're not soldiers. They don't understand war and why it is necessary to kill the other oaf and his kin and his generations and wipe him off the face of the earth forever and ever. They don't understand that oafs can't be changed, can't learn to do things a new way—blood must be spilled for the oaf to learn. Indeed, blood ever be the oaf's schoolmaster. No, she's not a spy. She's a talking man. And she's a musical man too. A combination like that—why, that makes her very expensive."

The others nodded at his wise words.

The oaf called Gen'rl said, "Give us another song, girl, if you can."

Her fingers touched the strings again. The others drew close as she played.

The oaf called Gen'rl said, "Back away from her. She's mine. The spoils of war. I'm taking her home to my children. And if this Luf'tnt Auutet, whoever he may be, has a problem with that, bid him come speak with me about it. Fi, fi, fi. Bid him come speak with me about it with his blade unsheathed."

The oafs backed away, and listened enchanted as the female man played their songs.

But her heart mourned. *Auutet. Auutet. You shall unsheathe your blade nevermore.*

In the early morning when it was still black, the oaf called Gen'rl would awaken and demand a song, and she would play.

She would be seated on his cot beside him, and he would feed her grains and pet her head as she played. He would nod his head, or mouth the words if it were a song he knew. "My children are going to love her," he would say.

The other oafs would utter their agreement.

Then he would rise from the cot, and with the assistance of the obsequious, low-ranking officer, don his tunic. The standard of the scarlet star on black was larger on his tunic than it was on the tunics of all the others, for he was their leader.

And Luf'tnt Auutet, *whoever he was*, never did appear with his blade unsheathed to speak with him about it.

At the completion of his early-morning toilet, he would go to the table with the other officers to gaze at the map and discuss the war, which was not progressing as swiftly or as well as they had hoped it would.

On the fourth day he said to the other officers gathered around the table, "We didn't see that one coming. It was quite unexpected indeed. They are scoundrels to have developed a counterattack such as that! But we proved our courage, I tell you. We took their best. They will never see a day like that again. We will seize the moment from them. We will dump them back on their haunches. We will beat them into submission, for our cause is the right and just cause and the words of great scripture our guide. Curses to the great leader!"

Then he announced that it was time to go check on the war, and he prayed: "Oh great creator, protect us as we do your will. And if we fall in battle, remember us evermore in your kingdom to come."

And they said, "Verily in your name!"

And he said, "Verily in your name!"

And he left the cave accompanied by his officers. From outside the cave came a great jangling of brass as the host of oafs trudged away. They were going to meet the war and would not return until the end of day.

She remained in the cave with the other captive mans. They were watched over by the one-eyed oaf, who turned out to be friendly and talkative.

And they were watched over by the one with three teeth in his mouth, who would occasionally eat one of them—but not her because she belonged to the one called Gen'rl, though now and again he would give her face a spit'ly lick to get the taste of her.

The one with three teeth in his mouth had a large appetite, a large belly, and a bad smell. He never strayed too far from his cooking instruments and the roasting spit. He always seemed to have a charred leg of man in his hand that he was nibbling on.

On that fourth day, while the one with three teeth in his mouth was salivating as he slowly turned a man roasting on the spit and the one-eyed one told him funny stories about his wife and children back home, she played the small singing harp to entertain them. She heard a whispered voice behind her: "Where can a man who has lost his way find a plate of food?"

Her fingers continued to glide over the strings, but she turned and saw a man.

He was a funny-looking man. He was a talking man, of course, but unlike any she had ever seen before. He was not wearing a brass tunic with a standard on it. He was not wearing colored cloths in his hair or a pouch around his loins. He was not wearing the long gray shirt of the mines. He was dressed like an oaf, in a shirt and pants.

He had shoes on his feet.

She did not know that they made shoes small enough to fit mans. She spent her formative years in a wealthy home and had never seen a man in shoes. Even the mans dressed as oafs for amusement at circuses never wore shoes. She kept looking at his feet. It was too much. She felt herself laughing and suppressed it, never missing a beat in the song she played.

"Well, Red," the man whispered, "where can I find a plate of food?"

Using her hips, she nudged her bowl to him.

He said, "Now that's a right friendly gesture."

The little man man came out from the shadows of the wall, but was careful to remain shielded by her body from the oafs in the cave. He quickly reached into her bowl, grabbed a handful of grains, and stuffed it in his mouth.

As he chewed, he said, "It's not much, but it will have to do."

She whispered, "Why are you here, little man?"

He leaned close to her ear. "I'm looking for loot. These fellows in here are loaded with silver."

"Money? Yes," she said, "the one called Gen'rl has some in his bag he keeps under his cot. I don't think the rest of them have anything. They're very poor. This is a war of the poor. But the one called Gen'rl is wealthy, though he leads the poor."

"And would you be so kind as to direct me to his cot?"

"You will get yourself killed," she warned. "You and your man shoes."

He had a sly look on his face. "You like my shoes?"

"They're funny," she said.

"Just point me to the cot of the wealthy one, and I will find a pair of shoes to fit even your feet."

"I wouldn't wear such obscene things."

"Point me to the cot then."

"Be careful."

"Point, Red, just point!"

"I'm sitting on it."

He dove under the cot. She heard jangling and became worried, but none of the oafs seemed to have heard it. None of the ailing ones stirred. The one-eyed one kept on talking, and the three-toothed one kept on turning the blackened corpse on the spit. The little man came back up from under the bed with a big grin on his face and pockets bulging with silver that jangled as he walked back into the shadows of the cave and then vanished from her sight.

Later, when the friendly one had finished talking, she rested the small singing harp on the cot and went to the back of the cave to investigate.

There was a low opening in the cave wall. It looked too small for her to squeeze through unless she got down on her face and completely flattened her body against the ground. But the funny-looking man was thinner than she was. He looked like a hungry one. And his master had taught him to steal. He was the man of a sneak thief. She had never met one of those before. She had grown up in the house of the wealthy and then in the house of the poor, but they were honest poor. And clean, not like these filthy oafs.

It has always been said that the quality of the oaf is reflected in the quality of his mans.

When the one called Gen'rl came back from the war that evening, he was in a dark mood and he demanded song.

So were they all in a dark mood, for it had not gone well for them that day.

They grabbed the mans that were bound by rope, about fifty of them, and swung their heads against the walls or crushed them with rocks or smashed them with clubs as the female man played their favorite songs, and then they did devour them.

She had no real love for these mans that they were devouring. She had never become friendly with them because most of them were weaklings who always cried to be returned to their masters when the work in the mines became too hard—but the smell of their blood made her head swing.

She missed a few beats in her song, which made the oafs gurgle with blood in their laughter. When they opened their mouths she saw pulverized skulls. When they closed their mouths their lips were red and glistening with viscera.

After he had eaten his fill, the one called Gen'rl came to the cot and looked at her with a dangerous fever, and she played the anthem for him over and over again until he calmed himself and fell asleep: "Justice vision, Justice true, fair to the unfair, Justice bleed . . ."

When she thought he was sleeping, she set the small singing harp on the ground and sighed, but his enormous arm shot up, grabbed her, and pulled her down.

He kissed her with lips pasted over with the sticky remains of the dead.

8

In Fever in War

War, war, war, do you know what war is?" the oaf called Gen'rl said, with his lips pursed against her face. "There is a village, and an oaf in that village owns a tree that bears sweet red fruit. The sweetest fruit to eat. Redder than red. Sweeter than sweet. We shall call this oaf Tlotl, for that is a common name. And in this village when the tree of Tlotl is full of fruit, he calls all of his friends who live in the village to eat of the fruit, for the village is small, and all of the oafs who live in it are his friends. Redder than red is the fruit. Sweeter than sweet. Everyone who eats of the fruit is happy. But Tlotl has a friend, and we shall call him Dlapna, for that also is a common name, and this parable represents all oafenkind. And Tlotl and Dlapna have an argument over trifles, a falling out. Dlapna holds a grudge against Tlotl, and Tlotl holds a grudge against Dlapna. Many moons pass during which they do not speak to each other. Then it is that time of year again when the tree of Tlotl becomes ripe with fruit and Tlotl calls all of his friends to come eat of the fruit, for the fruit are plentiful and the village is small, and all who live in it are his friends. They come to eat of the fruit of the tree of Tlotl, even

Dlapna, with whom Tlotl had the falling out. Redder than red is the fruit. Sweeter than sweet. Tlotl and his friend Dlapna eat of the fruit together, sharing fellowship and laughter. Neither can remember why it is they have not spoken these many moons. In fact, they have missed each other tremendously. The moral is this: trifles are easily forgiven when the fruit of the tree of Tlotl is in season. So it is in a small village where one oaf owns the tree of sweet fruit and the other has a wife that mends torn garments and another has a bovin that gives sweet milk and another has the gift of sharpening knives and another has the gift of bending shoes for hosses. An oaf cannot stay angry with his neighbor, for his neighbor brings too much goodness to his life. His neighbor is important in his life and he says good morning and good eventide to him each day. War is when Tlotl and Dlapna have a falling out over a trifle, and Dlapna can get his fruit at one of many markets. Then it is the blood of Tlotl and Dlapna and of their children that flows sweeter than sweet, redder than red, in the streets of their village. At least, that is how my father explained it to me when I was a boy. Good night, little mouse. Good night."

He kissed her again and he fell asleep. And she fell asleep with her face pressed against his lips.

His breath tasted like the corpse of man.

In the morning the one called Gen'rl said to those gathered around the map, "I have never deceived you, and I will not deceive you now. We have lost the mines. Our forces were outmaneuvered and we were forced into a temporary retreat. We have lost much ground, as you know, and the ground that we have lost cannot be retaken with the number we have here. This is not to say that we will not win the day. We will win the day, just not *this* day. Our mission this morning is to reinforce the western line. We will do our duty and we will do it well. The western line shall be held. And then tomorrow, we will return to the mines and we shall take them if it costs us our very lives."

They looked at him with determined eyes, each one nodding his head. *This we will do, for our standard is true.*

The one called Gen'rl said, "Let us pray. Oh great creator, protect us as we do your will. And if we fall in battle, remember us evermore in your kingdom to come!"

And they said, "Verily in your name!"

And he said, "Verily in your name! To arms, great oafen heroes!"

And he left the cave in the company of his officers.

The female man played her small singing harp, but the talkative one was not talkative today, and did not seem much interested in listening to music. He lay on his cot staring up at the ceiling with his single eye. Yesterday's battle had turned his mood.

It had turned the mood of the three-toothed one as well. He killed and ate no mans today. There was no fire under his spit today.

An hour or so after the others had left for the war, the three-toothed one and the once-friendly one-eyed one made their way over to the cot upon which she sat. They had words to say to each other out of earshot of the others.

"Fine officers we are. We are traitors."

The one-eyed one said, "Do you think he knows?"

The three-toothed one said, "Perhaps not, but it's only a matter of time. All fingers point back to us."

"But does he know?"

"If we don't get moving today, we'll be dead. They'll eat us like they eat mans."

The one-eyed one shook his head. "But I don't think he knows. It's a long ways to go, and the way is very treacherous. Bad weather is coming too. I would like a bit of certainty, if you don't mind."

"Waiting for certainty will get you killed. The old boy is no fool."

"Well, okay," said the one-eyed one, "how do we do this?"

The three-toothed one put up a finger for emphasis. "We leave. We leave *now*. We'll be across the border in three days."

"We just leave," said the one-eyed one, "without taking *anything*? The old boy has got silver under his cot, you know?" Then he tenderly touched the red-haired female man's cheek. "The advantage of the man on a long journey: loyal traveling companion, tireless beast of burden, and proper meal when nothing else avails." He gave her cheek a spit'ly lick and added, "Furthermore, she has to be worth a fortune."

"Take whatever you must," said the other. "But let's get out of here now."

They put the silver in a sack, and they put the sack under a cloak. The one-eyed one reached for her, and she chomped his hand.

"Ouch! I thought they said she was housebroken domesticated."

She tried to run, but the three-toothed one grabbed her before she could take a second step. She whipped her head around and tried to sink her teeth into him as he secured her arms and legs and mouth.

Then, muttering profanely, they put her in a sack too.

* * *

She felt that they were walking. They walked only a few paces before the sack in which she was borne fell to the ground. She heard noisy jangling and assumed that the sack bearing the stolen silver had fallen too.

The hands of the one called Gen'rl came into her sack and lifted her gently out and set her on the ground and removed the cloth that was tied over her mouth.

When she was out of the sack, she saw that the three-toothed one and the one-eyed one were bound in rope and lying on the ground. The entire host of oafen soldiers was gathered around them. The chant, "Spy, spy, spy, at the point of the sword, die, die, die!" was bouncing on everyone's lips.

She and the sack of silver were taken back into the cave and set down on the cot by one of the oafs, who rushed back outside so as not to miss the show.

Oafen soldiers, she had come to learn, took especial pleasure in watching someone else tortured. Only the weakest of those ailing and injured in the cave remained on their cots. All of the other ailing and injured found the strength to hobble out to see the torture of the two traitors.

Her ears were filled with their screams as the show began.

The mans in the cage slapped their hands over their ears so that they would not have to hear. Mans do not take pleasure in the suffering of anyone, not even their own tormentors.

"Hey, Red. Have you any food for a man who has lost his way?"

She turned. The funny-looking little man was back.

"What do you want now?" she said to him.

From outside, there came the whoosh as of a heavy chain being swung, followed by a soul-searing scream. The little man in the little oafen shoes smiled like music to his ears, then shot both hands into her bowl of grains.

"Food. That's the first thing," he said, swallowing fistful after fistful. Then he rubbed his stomach. "Better. Much better."

Without invitation, he opened the sack of silver on the cot next to her, reached in, and stuffed his pockets greedily with coin, and then said, "That's the second thing, and that's it for me," and dashed toward the opening at the back of the cave.

She shouted after him—shouted, but none of the ailing oafs on their cots took note of it because of the entertainment of the screams from outside. She shouted: "Who are you stealing that money for? He's going to get in trouble with the authorities, you know?"

His answer surprised her: "I'm stealing it for myself."

And he disappeared through the hole in the bottom of the cave wall.

She pondered this answer as the torture outside the cave continued. It lasted all day, for oafs are skilled at torture and can make it last all day.

At the end of the day, she assumed the traitors were dead because of the absence of screams, but she still did not have an understanding of the odd little man's strange answer to her question.

A man who steals for himself.

* * *

That evening, to celebrate the death of the traitors, the one called Gen'rl assembled the host of oafs outside before the fires and bid the two oafs of talent play their colored flutes, and the colors were blue for sky and red for blood and gray for hope.

And they played the Life Song of Great Lord Gerwargerulf.

And the one called Gen'rl came and sat beside the red-haired female man as she played on her small singing harp along with the poet and the players of the colored flute.

And the one called Gen'rl put his arm around the female man. She looked up at him and he looked down at her with fever in his eyes.

And the one called Gen'rl ordered that the large cage be emptied of mans.

The cage contained a hundred mans, and they emptied it. And then they emptied the mans of their lives through the brutish methods of the bashing of heads against stone and wood, as they had done the night before, and they did devour the mans with much noise and revelry.

She played through the monstrous festival of blood on her small singing harp the songs she used to play for the boy and his family when she was free, and it helped, though not a lot.

That night after it was all over, she lay on the cot with the one called Gen'rl, and he kissed her as though he were the oafen husband and she were the oafen wife, and that was the beginning.

He ripped off her tunic of war and had his way with her.

She wept all through it.

* * *

After his fever for her had been sated, he said, "You know how it ends, don't you?"

She knew, for she had seen it many times in the mines. Oafs always eat the mans they have ravished.

"I do not want to die. I want to live," she cried out. "Let me live, I pray, oh master. Oh great master, let me live."

And the oaf called Gen'rl did chuckle in his amusement. "But what is the life of a man?"

The red-haired female man pleaded for her life. "Is there no mercy in your heart?"

"You are beautiful, and I desire you in a way that is obscene. If I allow you to live I place myself in peril. I have committed a sin against earth and heaven."

"I will not tell."

"Hahaha. And what about these good oafs? Will they keep our secret too? Soldiers cannot keep such a secret." He held her close to his mouth and told her, "We are not the first, and we shall not be the last. There are oafs who have had offspring with mans. No one talks about it, but it is true and it does happen. I would not deceive you. I think we are the same species—we are just bigger, but I am not a scientist so I cannot swear to it, and the ones who have done this thing were put to death or banished and the offspring of their union sold for food. It is an especial meat and expensive. The poor cannot afford it, but I have eaten it many times, this offspring of oaf and man."

He touched her and she wept a large tear at his touch.

"It is delicious," he said.

He touched her again and she sobbed loudly.

"Yes, yes. This is indeed regrettable. Soldiers know of this. Soldiers do this all the time, but we do not talk of it. I am an old soldier, and it is a shameful act that I have committed. Tomorrow, after the victorious battle, I will slay and eat you. Don't think me cruel, for it is better than eating your own children, is it not? It will save us both the embarrassment."

And he rose up and bound her with rope next to him so that she could not escape. Then he lay back down.

Soon his lips were snoring against her weeping eyes.

That night, her mother came to her in a dream.

Her hair was red like a forest of fires. Her face was brown like the bark of a strong tree in the middle of the forest. And she was smiling a great and triumphant smile.

On her feet were shoes small enough for even a man to wear.

Then her mother, with the triumphant smile upon her face, climbed a great ladder and into the clouds disappeared from sight.

Despite all that had happened, the little female man was comforted by this dream because she understood it to mean: *The time has come. Their world shall pass away.*

9

Their World Shall Pass Away

In the morning the one called Gen'rl said to those gathered around the map, "Today we go to final victory. There is no turning back. This is the day we have been longing for. We are outnumbered, but we are not undone. Let us pray! Oh great creator, protect us as we do your will. And if we fall in battle, remember us evermore in your kingdom to come!"

And they said, "Verily in your name!"

And he said, "Verily in your name! To arms, great oafs!"

The female man was bound in rope on his cot. She was the last man alive in the cave, all the others having been devoured.

One of the ailing oafs was put to watch her, but he slept for most of the morning and then gasped loudly and finally on his cot, and he was dead.

She knew that he was dead because his chest was no longer wheezing. He was dead, but not from his ailing.

From behind the dead oaf appeared the strange little man, and the blade in his hand was red with blood. She looked again and saw that the oaf's throat had been cut clean through.

The strange little man wiped the blood from his blade with his shirt, and then he used it to saw through the rope that bound her. He told her, "Come with me if you want to live."

Brushing back tears, she said, "I want to live." And they raced to the hole at the back of the cave.

"Don't forget your harp," he told her.

She went back and got her harp and then he showed her how to flatten her body so that she could fit into the hole at the back of the cave, and then she followed him through the hole, and just in time.

She heard the soldiers loudly chanting their victory as they came back early from the battle that they had won: "Fe! Fe! Fe! Victory!"

She heard the one called Gen'rl cry hysterically, "She's gone! She's gone! Where has my little red-haired female man gone?"

As she ran ever deeper into the dark vault of space behind the cave, she heard one of the ailing ones say, "She went through a hole at the back of the cave, sir. There! See?"

She heard the tremendous hammer blows against the rock. She heard them breaking through the rock. There were harsh cries as the oafs came through the cave wall—coming after them.

"Fi! Fi! Fi! Die! Die! Die!"

She ran and she ran. There was no time to think or even to breathe. She raced after the little man through the winding recess at the back of the cave, and then, finally, there was light.

There was a hole in the hard ground and a light came up through it.

When she looked down into it, she saw a never-ending series of steps, a stairway that went down, down, down. But down to where?

"Fi! Fi! Fi!" sang the oafs behind them.

"Let's go!" urged the little man.

But despite the noise of huffing, puffing pursuit behind her, she refused to take a step down the lighted hole.

She was much too afraid.

"Fi! Fi! Fi!" sang the oafs.

The little man took her hand and spoke to her gently, and his voice had a calming effect on her fear. "It's okay. Don't be afraid. This is a hole in the firmament. You will be safe."

"What is a firmament?" she asked.

"Uhm, er," he said, "that's an explanation that will have to wait for a later date. Hurry, let's go!"

Holding her hand, he steadied her, and down she went.

She stepped into the hole in the firmament and stood stock still on a plank, a step that was as firm as solid ground. When she looked down, all she could see were stairs going downward, on and on. And below that, at the lowest level, the stairs were hidden in what looked like clouds.

It was a strange sensation staring down at clouds below her feet.

Then the little man also stepped into the hole with the stairs that led down to the clouds, and she watched him as he reached back up and pulled the cover into place and secured it from below.

"Fi! Fi! Fi!"

She cowered at the noise above their heads, but he told her, "Don't be afraid. Once that cover is pulled back into place, the portal becomes impossible to detect. They'll be marching over rocks and stones for hours, seeing nothing. It'll all look like rocks and stones to them."

They stood beneath the firmament and listened as the oafs lumbered over the hole, now hidden by its latched cover. They passed over it like thunder. And over it and over it and over it, they thundered.

"Fi! Fi!"

She pressed the heels of her hands against her ears to block out the noise of it. The terror of it. In time, the thunder stopped.

The end of it was a relief to her, and she said to him, "What if they had come through?"

He shrugged. "It has happened before."

"And?"

"I dealt with it." From inside his shirt, he withdrew an object such as she had never seen before in her life. It was a shiny black thing of peculiar shape, a kind of machine that he held in his fist the way a child holds a toy. "This is a pistol," he said. "It is a surefire giant killer. The last one that followed me through that hole went tumbling down those stairs after I slew him with this."

She nodded, though she did not understand how a toy could kill an oaf, and she imagined that he was boasting, for he did seem a boastful little man as well as an unsavory little sneak thief.

As she followed the sure-footed little man down the stairway to the clouds, down, down, down to she knew not where, she wondered again, *Who is he?*

As if reading her mind, he turned to her about two and a half zlazla hla-cubits down the stairs and he told her, "My name is Rufus."

"Oh."

"But you can call me Jack."

And down they stepped, down the winding and infinite stairs, until they reached the clouds, and beneath the clouds there was another firmament, and scattered over the broad plane of the lower firmament were the dead and broken bodies of several large oafs.

There were at least four dead and broken bodies that she could see.

Rufus who was called Jack laughed an embarrassed laugh as he explained, "I shot them with my little pistol and they came a-tumblin' down."

"This is carnage! I thought you said that you had killed but one!"

He blushed. "I lied."

"Obscene," she said. "You are no better than they are, Rufus who should be called Jack the liar!"

Rufus shook his head at her childish ideas as he reached down into the clouds and grabbed hold of a small ring, which he pulled. Up came the door in the floor, revealing another hole. But there was no bright light coming through this hole, only darkness.

Rufus said, "Here it is. This is the door to my world."

"But it is so dark," she said.

Rufus laughed at her ignorance.

"It is nighttime in my world, and we are entering it through the sky. We are high atop a great mountain, whose peak is hidden by clouds. Of course it is dark down there, but you are going to love it."

"But what is this? How is this?"

A thoughtful look settled upon his face. "God, I think. I think God did it—or as you say, the *great creator*. I think they were gods, once upon a time, maybe angels, and we built a tower to join them. But God—uhm, er, your great creator—put an end to it, and all that is left is this portal, these thousands and thousands of stairs."

"That's ridiculous," she said.

He shrugged. "Well, it's just a theory." Then he scratched his chin and added, "You know, Red, I'm not just a world-class adventurer and explorer. In my world I am a professor, a teacher at a university—what they would call in your world the *great school*—and I hold degrees in many subjects, including history, religion, and linguistics."

She said, "You're a sneak thief and a rascal is what you are."

He muttered under his breath an unheard thing: "Just like a human. Free for less than a day, and already she takes her freedom for granted. Already she has forgotten the one who brought her out of bondage. She will do well in my world."

"What's worse," she continued, "you have no respect for life."

"The life of an *oaf*?" he said. "They enslaved you and would have eaten you as food."

"All life is life," she said.

"Even that of your enemies?"

"Even that of my enemies. There is much good in them too," she said, remembering her boys. The one who risked his life to rescue her. The one she so longed to see.

He muttered under his breath another unheard thing: "We will see, Red. We will see."

And then once again he took the hand of the barefoot red-haired girl and steadied her as she stepped down into the dark hole that led to his world.

Thus did the female man enter the world of man.

10

Mans of the Snow

And if the man has dreams, these dreams be of oafen bliss and visions of heaven.

—Great Scripture

When I was a little boy, my mother and father took me to the zoo. They took me to see the lions, and that was okay. They took me to see the tygas, and that was okay. They took me to see the great serpents, and that was okay. They took me to see the olyphants, and that was okay. They took me to see the mans of the snow, and that was the best because every time I went to the zoo, I wanted to see what new kind of mans they had brought in because I love mans. In my opinion, man is the greatest animal on earth and everybody should have one as a pet.

Now, the mans of the snow I saw in the zoo that day were different from all the other mans I have ever seen before, and I have seen a lot of mans. There are mans who live in the forest, and they are really small and their skin is a very dark color to blend in with the leaves. There are mans who live on the plains, and they have almost no hair on their bodies.

There are mans who live in the mountains, and they have long colorful body hairs, long legs, and tiny light-colored eyes. Amazing as these mans are, the mans of the snow are different from all of them.

The mans of the snow are not as tall as most other mans, and they are fairly plump. My teacher says the extra fat is to keep them warm and their pale color is to help them blend in with the snow so that other predators as well as prey can't see them coming. Unlike other mans, the mans of the snow make actual clothes. They hunt the great white beos and use their hides to protect against the freezing cold. On their feet, they wear the hide of beo like primitive shoes to protect from the snow. And when they remove their shoes, you notice that their feet are different from all other mans on earth—they cannot grasp with their feet, for their feet have no thumbs. In that respect, their feet are similar to our own.

The other thing that makes the mans of the snow different from all other mans is that they are the greatest hunters of all. The people at the zoo brought in a great white beo and we watched as the mans of the snow hunted it. The people in the zoo did not let them actually kill the beo, but we got to see them preparing their tools for the hunt, setting up in attack formation, and then launching their spears. One spear hit the beo and he growled a mighty growl and then they brought down a wall between the two cages so that the mans couldn't hurl any more spears at it. The mans of the snow are very exciting to watch at a zoo, and it would probably be great to own one as a pet, but they are very expensive.

Even though my parents are not wealthy, I am fortunate that I have owned three mans in my life. My first man was not really mine and I had to give him back. My second man was a musical man and a fighting man, and I loved her very much, but she died. Now I own the best man of all.

She has red hair, she is musical, and I know this will be hard to believe, but she is a talking man. Sometimes she and I argue over things because she has strong opinions. I have only had her for six months, but we do everything together and go everywhere together. We are best friends. We will be best friends forever. I never knew I could love anything so much.

In conclusion, I am so happy that I have a man. She is fun to play with. Her music is fun to listen to. She is fun to talk to when she is not being sarcastic. My life has improved a lot since she came into it. I think every child should have a man.

11

Red Locks

Now listen, Red Locks," the boy told his female man. "I'm going to read something I wrote about you."

"About me?"

He showed her the paper. "I wrote it for school."

"Why me?"

"Because I love you," he said. "You are my favorite thing in the whole world."

"Then by all means, you should read it to me," she said.

The boy began to read.

And she listened, enraptured.

12

The Oaf

The boy grew up and was a boy no more.

The boy grew up and became a full-grown oaf, as was his father and his father's father before him.

He was wed and started a family. And times were hard, so he and his young family were forced to remain with his parents.

For a time, they said.

And one year became two, and two became four, and four became eight, and ten years later, ten regular years, he was still going to bed and waking up in his childhood room, though he had a wife and somewhere scattered around the house were his two children.

He thought often about the mans of his childhood. He thought about them every night, despite all that had happened and how things had changed.

One night in his bed he lay awake thinking about his mans, and there came a persistent tapping on his window. He arose and there was a man looking inside the window at him—a female man with red hair, green eyes, and frecks.

Frecks and wrinkles.

In regular years she would be eighteen. In man years she would be fifty-four.

He rushed out into the backyard and hugged her so tight she begged him to release her, and he did. And then she hugged him back and seemed unwilling to let him go.

She said, "I missed you so."

The boy who was now an oaf said, "And I missed you."

In the yard with her were three other mans and an odd-looking little oaf that he had never seen around these parts. She introduced everybody but the oaf, who looked to be a simpleton. She said, "This is my husband Rufus, but everyone calls him Jack. This is my son Bob, and this is my daughter Janet." And then she told them, "This is my old master, Zloty. He was the best master I ever had."

He shook all of their little hands and then hugged them all, including Rufus who could also be called Jack.

"Zack?"

"No, I'm Jack," said Jack. "Adventurer, scholar, and giant-killer at your service."

Zloty shrugged, for he did not understand. Then he eyed the pinhead oaf again to see if maybe he knew him, and again it was nobody that he knew.

And then he thought, *It is dangerous these days for mans to travel through the streets. It is illegal for them to be out and about without a leash or an escort. So many of them have been killed. So many of them have been stolen. In this neighborhood, so many of them have been stolen and made into a meal. If the scientists don't work fast, all of the free-range mans will be dead. The swamp of the Eternal Grass has already dried up. In the north, the great white beos are gone and the ice caps are melting. So maybe this pinhead with them is someone she met after being stolen from me, and she contacted him first and made him her escort so that they all could pass through the streets without worrying about the authorities.*

But the oaf was rather short for an oaf, standing a little less than three hla-cubits, while the oaf Zloty, who was considered slightly below average in height by oaf standards of his day, stood four and a half hla-cubits. The pinhead, Zloty figured, was just a little bit taller than a boy at the start of puberty, which made him a *very* short adult male oaf. And he had frecks on his face and arms, which was very unusual for an oaf. In ancient days, frecks were believed to be a sign of bad fortune and the infant born with them was strangled by its parents after its first suckle to please the great creator.

Her family moved to the other side of the backyard to give her some time alone with her old master. She explained to him all that had transpired since she had been stolen from him. She explained to him the new world in which they lived.

"It is a long, long journey that can only be made by foot. We are separated from your world by about 70,000 zlazla hla-cubits of stairs, but in many ways our world is much like yours. We have war, poverty, racism, sexism, religious intolerance, crime—we are destroying our natural environment."

He asked her to explain religious intolerance.

"You will not understand it because in your world you only have one religion."

"What is religion?"

"As I said, in your world everyone believes in the great creator. In the world of mans, people believe many different things."

"How can they believe many different things?"

"It is hard to explain."

Then he asked her to explain racism, which translated poorly into his language as *hatred of the difference in the hue of the fruit on a single branch.*

She struggled for the words to explain. "Well, as you can see," she said, "my husband Rufus has dark skin and my skin is pale."

"Frecked," he corrected.

"Well, okay, but see, Rufus and I are considered to be from different races, uhm, er, from different family trees, understand? And this causes a problem for some people down there."

He snorted. "You are pulling my leg, right? I'm no pinhead. You come from the same *racing fruit tree*, or whatever you call it. You are both mans. A little female man and a little man man."

They both laughed at that but for different reasons; he at the truth in it, and she for the irony of it.

Then since she had mentioned that in her new world she was wealthy and he had always dreamt of being wealthy, he asked, "So how do you earn your money in your world? What do you do for a living, little wealthy man?"

She said, "Nothing. Rufus comes and steals silver from your world every few years."

"Aha, silver is money in your world too." For some reason this pleased him. Perhaps because at last here was a thing he understood. Their worlds had something in common—the love of silver.

"I arrived in that new world with wealth. Silver is worth money there, but so is a substance called gold. Gold, in your world, is used to make rope and thread. It is found in most cloth. The hair cloths I went there with were worth a fortune. My loin pouch also. The tunic of war that I wore was lined with it. And the small singing harp I was given by one of the evil soldiers I told you about who owned me before I left—it too was made of pure gold. Your mother's singing harp would be worth a fortune in my world. In my world you and your family would be wealthy because of that small singing harp alone, which in your world is regarded as the least significant of instruments."

They talked about many other things, but eventually she asked him, "What has happened to this world? It used to be so vibrant, so green. It looks like a desert everywhere we've been. Was it the war? Who won the war?"

He said, "Which war? It has been ten years of wars. There have been four wars in ten years. I fought in one of these."

Shaking his head sadly, he pulled up his pant leg to show her the scar, as winding and ugly as the one on her arm.

"Nobody ever wins a war. A new one is starting right now, but it is of no concern to us. A war changes nothing for the poor, except that if you are the right age you fight in it and die. And my friend Auutet, my best friend in the whole wide world and your first master, though he was wealthy, he was also noble and earnest and good; and he did fight on the side of the poor in the war and was killed in battle. My heart still aches for him."

Auutet. Auutet. Her heart did ache as well, but in silence as the boy of her childhood spoke.

"This desert, as you call it, is because we are going through a worldwide famine. This happens in a cycle every few thousand years—oafenkind has been on earth for 10,000 years. It is nothing to worry about. Things will get better. We will survive."

"Oh."

He lowered his voice. "That is what the wealthy say . . . but our sacred speaker says there are people, scientists, who believe that it signals the end of days."

"What do you mean?"

"They say we have angered the great creator and he has turned his back on us and left us to perish in a world that we have destroyed. We have poisoned the air with our mining and the waters with our waste, we have scorched the face of the earth with our overharvesting and our wars. We have caused the cold places to become warm. Many animals have died and will never return. The free-range mans are almost all gone. There are almost no more mans in the wild. We have hunted them into near extinction. The only mans alive now are mans that we raise for pets and circuses."

She frowned. "Pets and circuses."

"I do not mean to hurt your feelings."

"I know. You are a good oaf."

"I remember you told me that your mother said this world was going to die. But I do not think I believe it. The great creator would not give the oaf the power to destroy the world. The oaf is but a part of the world. The oaf is a creature of nature too. If the oaf overhunts an animal and it dies out, then that is a natural death because the oaf is a natural creature too."

"True, but the great creator gave the oaf understanding," she argued, "which makes him greater than other natural creatures. The oaf, unlike other creatures, *understands* that he is destroying the world for a selfish and temporary purpose, and he is able to correct his actions and halt the destruction. If he does not do that, then maybe he is indeed but a dim-witted pinhead and does not deserve to be called the greatest of the great creator's creations, right?"

She saw from his expression that he lacked understanding. There was a chasm between them that she could not bridge. But he was soooooo big. She had forgotten how big he was. How big and how handsome.

They looked at each other, and there was something that he wanted to tell her and there was something that she wanted to tell him.

It was she who spoke first.

He knelt close and she whispered into his face: "I have learned of a thing that I did not know before. The way I learned it was painful . . . but now I understand some things about us, you and me. We are not different beings, your people and mine. We come from the same family tree. We are the same people, just different sizes. Man is but a smaller version of the oaf. And there is no such thing as talking mans and mans that cannot talk. Mans that cannot talk are simply mans who speak a different language."

She saw the look on his face and she knew he was about to ask a question, and she raised a hand for him to be silent.

"You do not know of languages because your people only have one language. So you do not even have a name for the language you speak. You do not even have a word for the word *language*." She paused to look at his eyes. Did he have understanding? Was it even worth it to keep trying to explain? "In my world," she went on, "your language would be called Frisian, which is not too different from the language I speak with my husband and my family, which is called English. My husband, who is learned among the mans of our world, speaks English, Frisian, French, Dutch, and German. These are languages. In my world, mans have many languages . . ."

She wanted to tell him that in many ways the humans of her world, and even the mans of his world, were more advanced than the oafs, who lived mostly clumped in large, overpopulated groups instead of spreading out and expanding their civilizations into the wildernesses and other continents of their world. The oafs, who possessed an almost religious fear of the unknown, had a belief that wildernesses were for hunters, adventurers, and scientists, but not for building cities in. Most oafs believed that wildernesses, along with forests, deserts, and mountains, were for plundering and bringing stuff back from, but not for living in. As a result of having lived so close together for such a long time, the oafs had never had their language or their blood stretched out and then comingled. They all looked alike and sounded alike, even when they were mortal enemies facing off in their many and devastating wars.

She continued: "Even in your world, mans have many languages, but only those fortunate enough to have grown up with oafs and who therefore speak the language of the oaf are considered to be talking mans. But all mans are talking mans, just as all oafs are talking oafs! Don't you understand? My mother was a talking man. She simply did not speak your language."

He nodded his head out of politeness, though he found it unbelievable that all mans were talking mans.

This new world that she had escaped to had filled her head with some very strange notions—this new world where mans could marry and be called *husband* and *wife*. Hahaha. Could there be such a place? Would the great creator allow such an impossible, upside-down place to exist? A world where mans wore shoes? He tried to picture it in his head, but it was too much like a story for children.

Hahaha.

There was no understanding in him at all.

She continued: "We are the same beings, you and I, so we can have feelings for each other that are greater than master and pet. Thus . . . you were my first love."

At last, there was understanding in his eyes.

"I was jealous when you fell in love with that girl, the one with the wicked brother who burgled me and sold me into the mines. But I am happy to know that I loved you. I used to think that it was a monstrous feeling I had for you, but now I know better."

He nodded his head, but was unable to speak the words—to say that he had loved her too. They had come of age at around the same time, but she was a lesser creature, a pet, and the ideas that he'd had in his head about her back then—they were monstrous, as she had said, simply monstrous. How he had wished for her to leave his room and go live in her proper kennel that he and his father had built with their own hands, but if she had done that then he would have spent all of his time out there with her because he had indeed loved her.

Yet he did not say this, and there was no need for him to say it because she was his elder and she knew these things through having lived an unsheltered and precarious life. He was bigger, but she was wiser, having traveled widely in both the old world and the new. Thus, she was his master.

But he was big and, oh, magnificently beautiful. She gazed unabashedly.

He joked, uncomfortably, under her gaze, "In your world, I see they make shoes small enough for mans!"

It was enough to break the spell. "You silly pinhead!" she said, shaking her head.

"Hahaha," he laughed.

"And," she whispered to him, "that one there, the simpleton." She pointed to the oaf. "He is Mike. He is my son from that oaf general I told you about who had his way with me."

He looked at the little pinhead again, and then he understood all things. *The frecks*, he laughed to himself. *The frecks*!

"He has frecks like his mother," he told her. Then he laughed out loud. "He is such a little thing for an oaf. What a shorty! Hahaha. They would tease him in school."

"But in our world, he is considered quite big. And you are so big, Zloty. I had forgotten just how big you are, and so handsome," said she to him.

"Oh," said he to her.

His blush was interrupted as just then his mother, Gretjel, looked through the window as did his father, Uulfnoth, and they recognized their red-haired female man. She had returned to them! They came outside, running with arms outstretched.

His children were there, his boys, Tado and Zloty the younger, and his wife who was named Gretjel, as was his mother, but was called Grietjelaia so there would be no confusion.

They all came out and embraced and exchanged stories.

And all were happy with joy and wonderment.

Just before his female man and her family made their return to their world, they lined up and in perfect harmony sang a beautiful song for the boy of her childhood and his family.

And then they sang more songs, and they too were beautiful, for her family was made up of all singing mans, even the oaf, whose name was Mike, a big simpleton, who had the beard and sexual maturation of a twenty-four-year-old man, but the mind and manner of an eight-year-old oaf, for he was both man and oaf.

Gretjel, the mother, ran inside the house and brought out a new small singing harp, as the first was destroyed during the burgling of their home that originated the adventure, and gave it to their long-lost and now returned female man, and she took it.

She bowed to Gretjel. "Thank you," she said.

Her husband Rufus had eyes that smiled and hands that rubbed together with glee when he saw the gift of the golden harp, which was priceless in their world. More wealth! *There can never be too much wealth*, he thought.

But his female man wife nudged him and he reached into his pockets, stuffed to bursting with stolen loot, and withdrew all the silver that he had nabbed earlier that day from a miserable old pinhead who lived in the caves near the hidden entrance to the portal between the higher and lower firmaments.

Rufus bowed graciously and gave the silver coins to Gretjel, the elder.

"Thank you," she said, bowing in her turn. "But this is too much. We are simple people. We do not need this."

Her husband Uulfnoth, whose eyes had smiled and whose hands had rubbed together with glee when he saw the silver being placed in his wife's hands, shook his head with great energy and hurriedly spoke these words: "What my wife is trying to say is that she is grateful for your most kind and most generous and most thoughtful gift, which we are most honored to accept." And he took the silver from his wife Gretjel's hands and stashed it with a quickness in his pockets.

Everyone smiled knowingly.

After the tearful goodbyes were spoken, the female man and her family made the long journey back to the lighted hole in the firmament, and they descended the many thousands of stairs on what remained of what once may have been a tower built by mans who wanted to join with the gods, and they returned home to their world and all of its problems.

And they were happy.

And her boy, who had become a full-grown oaf with boys of his own and an oafen wife who shared his mother's name, went back to his bed in his childhood home.

And he was happy.

And on the last day there shall come fire everlasting, and all things in the earth shall be burned, and then great heaven shall rain down her tears as on the first day when all things were born.

—Great Scripture

13

JACK

Jack made two final trips up to the realm of the oaf. He traveled both times with his stepson, the man-oaf Mike, who as he aged had become less simple and was beginning to show signs of true wisdom. Now at long last they understood that because he was part oaf, his cognitive development had only been delayed and not completely absent as they had previously thought.

The first trip took place six years after the triumphant journey with his wife and family—six years for the man, but only two years for the oaf. Jack returned from the first trip greatly disturbed, despite the large bag of silver he had pilfered.

He was troubled by what he had seen above the firmaments, and he would not talk about it.

A week passed. Then two. Finally his wife, whom he called Rose because of her red hair, pressed him hard until he said to her, "Zloty's wife is dead. One of his sons is dead. It has been a year of winter. Winter has lasted for a year, but it is beginning to thaw. All of the crops are dead. It was a year with no spring, no summer, no fall. The poor have suffered the worst of it. Zloty's parents are both ailing. He sent a message for you, and the message is this:

The conversation that we had when you visited remained in my head for a long time after you left, and I began to see signs that reminded me of your warning—not the deaths of my beloved wife and my beloved firstborn, but signs in great nature. You said that unlike other creatures, the oaf understands that he is destroying the world for selfish reasons and that if he were to correct his actions, he might halt the destruction. Are we destroying the world? Well, there is this present year of ceaseless winter. I have heard say that the wildernesses are flooded and that the rain is headed to the cities. This is destruction, is it not? But is it worldwide? Who is to say? Nevertheless, I would try to do something about it. So I united with several like-minded companions and we campaigned for an audience with the great leader, who after many months and much agitation on our part agreed to meet with us. He listened politely and with great patience about our need to mend our ways, to apologize to great nature by putting things back the way they used to be, and afterward he gave us assurances that if we did not end our fascination with these doomsday prophecies, he would have us arrested and severely punished. Well, I have another son at home and my parents to care for, so I relented. Now, do not you despair over us. The oaf is strong. We will survive. We also are a part of great nature. We are natural creatures. The great creator does not hate us. This is not his punishment of us for our wickedness and our indulgences. As the great leader and his advisors said, "Though for us it may be the last day, for the earth, it is not the end of days. For the earth, it is but a dark day."

With tears in her eyes, Rose cried, "That's it? That's the message?"

"That is the entire message," Jack said.

Jack's final trip took place six years after that last one—six years for the man, two years for the oaf—and when he and his stepson the man-oaf returned, he would not speak of the trip at all, no matter how hard his wife pressed him.

He surrendered to her the large bag of silver and the bag of gold that was twice the size of the silver, and he told her, "We shall live out the rest of our days on these bags. We are wealthy for the rest of our days and all the days of our children, but I shall nevermore return to that world and I shall nevermore speak of it."

It was the son, the man-oaf Mike, who told her about that final journey to the world above the firmaments.

He said, "The oceans cover the face of the earth. What little dry land exists is overrun with rats and other vermin, and their hunger is great. Where are the bovins and hosses and dogs and cats? Under the water. The sun is overly hot. Even the stars shine too hot. The ocean boils. To journey in the heat of the day is to risk death by fire. Better to journey at night. Life? We found a few mans piloting a boat and rode with them to see what was left of the world. They shared their food with us and we our provisions with them. Their meals were harvested from the sea—fish and the green weed that floats on the surface. We saw no birds while we were there. It is a world without birds. We asked the mans—for they were talking mans—where the cities and villages were. *Under the sea*, they told us. Charting our course by the stars, we rode with the mans to the place where your master Zloty once lived. The place where your master Zloty once lived was covered by the ocean. There was nothing for the eye to see but water. We sailed to a small island that was not covered by water, and the mans had set up a village there, but the water was rising. The man in charge told us, *You may not believe this, but this is the very peak of a great mountain, not an island, and soon, in a year, maybe two, it shall be covered. We shall have to find another place, or live forever on the boat*. On the island, they had silver and gold which they did give to us, for mans know not the value of silver and gold. In fact, the mans cursed the silver and the gold, believing that they were somehow to blame for the demise of their world, though they could not explain specifically how. After a few days, they returned us to the top of another high mountain—the same that has the cave in which the portal between the worlds is hidden. It must have been high tide. When we had arrived there in that world a few days before, the cave atop that mountain was dry land. But now as we were departing, the cave floor was covered with the ocean up to and over Jack's head and so I carried him on my back through the cave and to the portal. We went through and managed to close the firmament door above us, but water gushed through it, raining down on our heads as we descended the stairs. It was a thing I never wish to see again. A world as it passes away. A world that is dying."

"The day of the oaf is at an end," Rose said, bitterly weeping. "Mother was right. Oh, fi, fi, fi, she was right."

14

MIKE

When Mike reached the age of 119 and a half, he weighed a slim 302 pounds. He had never been a big eater and thus had always kept his weight down: he stood 9'6".

He was 119 in man years, which was the age of forty or so in the reckoning of the oaf. He had the appearance of a very tall, powerfully built gentleman of middle-age years with a full red beard. He walked with a back that was erect and proud despite his years, for as an oaf, he was still in the first third of his life.

As an oaf in the world of oafs, he would have been called *shorty*.

Down here, they called him *big man*, listed him in *Guinness*, wrote textbooks and newspaper articles about him. A marvel of nature. A mystery of science. Ageless. A big *oaf*—and that last was not said as a compliment. It was said because he had never been able to excel at the sport of basketball—never been able to excel at any sport despite his gift of great size.

Solitude suited him. There were too many questions down here, and he didn't like being a celebrity anyway—too many cameras, too many reporters, too many questions.

And his family was gone—mother, stepfather, brother, sister, and even the son[†] that he loved—fi, fi, fi, the life of man is so brief.

And so Mike moved to the mountain to think—to the mountain, whose snowy peak touched the clouds that hid the portal between his world and theirs.

His home was on the mountain, and he had lived there three years, three man years, one oaf year, before he made up his mind to see his plan through to the end.

He had decided at last that he was more oaf than man, even though that other world had passed away. He had been there with his stepfather on that last trip through the portal so many years ago. He had wept when he saw the devastation, because even back then, in the back of his mind, he had lodged the plan to remain there forever.

Before he had crossed through the portal, he had been planning to tell his stepfather these words at the end of their silver conquest: *Now, you go back to Mother and brother Bob and sister Janet and tell them that the big boob loves them, but he just does not fit. I just do not fit, Father. I am a freak in that world of yours and I am not going back. I will remain up here with those of my own kind, and I am changing my name to Tlotl. You and Mother will just have to learn to deal with it.*

And Mike, who wanted to be called Tlotl, knew that his stepfather, a wise and reasonable man, would have understood and supported his decision.

Jack would have nodded and said, *Just help me get that silver back*

---

†. See Apocrypha, page 165.

through the portal, kid, and you do what's best for you. I'll tell your mom. She'll learn to deal with it. We'll come up and see you from time to time. Don't you worry about us. Live your life the way you see fit.

Instead, when they got up there, the world of the oaf was in its death throes, and his dreams of living in a place where he was not a freak, but a common oaf with a common name, were gone forever.

So he married a woman and tried to live a normal life. The only good that came from that was his son, and now the son was gone, having inherited from his mother that peculiarly human disease called *short lifespan* and succumbed to it at age eighty-one (in man years).

The life of a man is so brief.

The life of an oaf is so long and so lonely.

But here on this mountain, the lonely, loveless, companionless freak had developed a final plan. He would go through the portal one last time and die up there.

It is fitting that my bones should rest up there. I shall set out swimming in the great eternal ocean and swim until the strength leaves my body and I surrender my life to the murky deep.

He reached up and found the secret latch to the door into the lower firmament and he opened it and pulled himself up and in.

He rested on the bottom rung of the nine miles of stairs and tugged thoughtfully on his long red beard as he gazed at his strange surroundings. All he could see were clouds on the ground, and jutting up out of the carpet of clouds here and there were the well-preserved corpses of the several oafs Jack had slain with his pistol so many years ago.

He sighed, memories. Memories. Fi, fi, fi.

Then he began to climb the stairway to the upper firmament. And he climbed and he climbed, and he did not stop for a rest. When he reached the top of the stairs, he stopped to say a prayer: "Lord and creator, be with me as I return to the sacred dust that made me. Amen."

Then he sang a song that his mother used to play on her small singing harp: "In the heart, in the air, hear the joy everywhere. Shall we call, shall we sing, of the joy everywhere? Come, my friends, let us sing, of the joy everywhere. There is joy, there is joy, there is joy everywhere."

"I have no friends," he said aloud, "but I have joy, dear lord."

And he undid the latch on the door through the upper firmament and he opened the door, bracing himself for the rushing flood of waters which would likely knock him off the stairs and send him tumbling down to his death, his body as broken and lifeless as the quietly resting corpses of the oafs that Jack had slain with his pistol.

But there was no water rampaging down through the door in the upper firmament.

"I guess it is low tide. I got lucky," the man-oaf mused as he pulled himself up to the hole in the firmament and then climbed into it.

He made it through the many tunnels. He made it to the cave. The cave was dark as always, but the ground was dry. There was no water beneath his feet.

"Low tide," he said again. "Am I not the fortunate oaf?"

In the cave, which was bereft of life except for his, he had another moment of reflection.

"This is the place where I was conceived. This is the place where that vile oafen general took advantage of my mother."

He left the cave, and the sun outside was bright, so bright that it took his eyes many minutes to adjust.

"The sun is still so hot," he said, and he was momentarily seized by the fear that he might die of fire before reaching the ocean, but when his vision had cleared his skin felt no pain and he saw that he was on a green mountaintop.

Green.

There were trees and grass and flowers in bloom. He looked, he looked and looked, but there was no sight of water.

"Perhaps the floods have receded."

On he walked, until he found the path that led down the mountain. Every step he took, he became more hopeful. His heart was filled with hope. He saw small animals scurrying up the trees. He heard insects buzzing. He heard birds singing.

There was a moment of real fear when he spotted two large brown beos blocking his path down the mountain. But he knew that beos were only dangerous if you troubled their cubs, so he waited a respectful distance away from them until they lumbered out of the way, followed by two lively, playful cubs that had been hiding among the trees.

"It is a good thing that I waited."

It took him half a day to make it down the mountain, and before he got to the bottom he spotted the village.

There were about a dozen houses and twice as many barns. He noticed six bovins penned into a yard and three hosses tethered to a post. He heard the happy yipping of a small dog. Someone—a young girl, a child, from the voice—was humming a merry tune.

His heart swollen with glee, he skipped the rest of the way down the mountain and then bounded toward the village, which was still about a mile away.

Now he could hear the sound of many dogs barking, large dangerous dogs this time. He heard more voices—male voices, adult males, and the voices were the voices of alarm.

There was the sound of a bell tolling. Sharp commands were shouted. He heard the words, "Giant! Giant! Arrow from quiver! Sword from sheath!"

He heard the unsheathing of swords.

He heard the angry hiss-whistle of arrows in flight.

The first arrow bit into his hand like a great and very sharp tooth.

The second one pierced his upper thigh, and his leg buckled beneath him and he fell.

He was close enough now to see that the houses of the village were too small for oafen habitation. This was a village of mans.

There was the sound of angry barking and the shocking pain of being violently ripped to pieces. The dogs were upon him in the pungent stink of their fury, their hungry mouths dripping warm, blood-tinged saliva, their razor teeth shredding flesh.

Beyond the black fur cloud of canine frenzy, he saw mans with their swords raised high, their heavy armor clanking. Now there was a sandaled foot upon his throat, and he squinted up at the bright sunlight reflected in the broadsword whose deadly edge was poised to deliver a deathblow and behead. Now there was the shout of

"Monster!" from the rumbling voice of the brave warrior—the brave giant killer looming above him.

"I am a man! I am a man!" he shouted frantically in Frisian, then English, then Dutch, then Swedish, then German—

There was a moment when he thought he would surely die, but then the noble giant killer rumbled another command and the dogs were pulled off and the biting ceased.

"The world survived the way it has always survived," the sacred speaker of the mans said in a language they called *Deutschailai*, which was a mixture of German, Old Frisian, and English. Mike, a student of language as had been his stepfather before him, found that he could communicate in Deutschailai with very little difficulty. "The storms washed away the old, and the new grew back in its place. We do not know why it happened or how it fixed itself, but the waters began slowly to recede after ten years, though it was a slow process. The plants came back shortly thereafter. My people with what animals they could take lived on boats and rafts and anything that would float during the ten years of the great waters and then the forty years of the lesser waters that followed. I was born on a boat and did not leave it until I was well into my middle years. The first time I set foot on land that was not a small island was when I was forty-five, and now I am sixty."

Mike, the man-oaf, sat at the head of the great table, a place of honor, and listened to the words of the sacred speaker of the mans. Mike wore the bloody bandages of his recent injuries on his hands, legs, and face. The dogs that had bitten him earlier now begged for scraps at his feet.

"The giants," the sacred speaker said, eyeing Mike curiously, "some of them survived it too. But they are not like they were before. There is no understanding in them. They have no civilization. They roam the world making mischief for all mans. They are cannibals. They seek not to befriend. They want only to eat us. We kill them if we can. We must, for they are monsters. And you look so much like them, though now that we see you up close—you are a man as we are, but a man of great size and wondrous frecks."

"The world survived." Mike nodded. "It survived, despite what they did to it."

"The world always survives," the sacred speaker said. "The world will survive despite what you do to it. But it is you who may not survive what you do to it. If you are used to living in a green forest and you chop down its trees and turn it into a desert, you will die because you cannot live in a desert. But the desert will become home to those of the great creator's creatures that can live in a desert. We mans love the way the world is, so we are careful not to do things to make it change into a world that we do not love. Thus, man, who is at one with his environment, shall inherit the earth. The oaf, on the other hand, is selfish, thoughtless, and careless in his actions. Now his world is lost. He had no respect for the natural world and now the natural world has no respect for him. He is a vagabond on the face of the earth. His day is at an end."

Mike, the man-oaf, nodded his head in understanding, and broke bread with the Deutschailai-speaking mans of the valley below the mountains.

And because he could not go back to the world of his birth where he was a freak, and because this world could not go back to the way it was before, Mike made a home with the mans of the valley below the mountains and lived with them for the rest of his days, which were long compared to the days of mans.

Mike lived to be an oaf of eighty-five, which is close to 255 in man years, and he was buried with the respect and love of all the mans of his village and the lands beyond, for he was great and wise in his deeds unto them.

There were those who believed him to be a god, and others who believed him to be an oaf, though Mike denied the oaf charge vehemently throughout his long life with them, for he loved them and did not want to be viewed as a monster. And so he would tell them that he came from the mountaintop, where he had hidden to escape the years of the great floods.

They knew the old stories and in good-natured jest they would refer to him as *Oaf Man* or *Great Oaf Mike* or *Gerwargerulf*.

Mike chafed at the nicknames, for oafs in those latter days had become monstrous indeed. They had resorted to a diet almost exclusively of meat (chicken, goat, hog, hoss, bovin, beo, dog, cat, rat, and man-meat whenever they could get it), and while they were becoming fewer and fewer in number, they were becoming larger in size.

The average height of these solitary hunters—who had lost the understanding of what it meant to be civilized people living in organized groups in villages and cities—the average height of these latter-day oafs was close to six hla-cubits (13'10"–14'), which was a full quazihla-cubits (about two feet) taller than what they had averaged in the days before the great flood.

It was not unusual for a skilled giant killer to discover and then bring down a behemoth of seven or even eight hla-cubits.

The record, however, was held by a pesky pinhead who measured over ten hla-cubits (23'9"–24'). This big oaf, an unrepentant goat thief and child snatcher, was active in his mischief for almost three years (oaf years) before being brought down by a young giant-killer from Mike's village.

The demise of this great oaf was a bittersweet event for Mike, for the behemoth was one whom Mike had encountered on occasion and whose personality he had found to be agreeable. In fact, Mike had considered him something of a friend, and it was he of whom Mike had once asked: "Do you remember how it was before the flood?"

And the great oaf had knit up his brow in oafish thought and said, "I remember that I lived in a house. I remember that I had a wife and that I loved her, I think. I do not know if there were children. I remember living in a village, and that there were many of us. I had a respectable profession, I know, but I cannot remember what it was. I think I worked with numbers, though now I have forgotten how to count as well as to read. I remember water, year after year of water, water everywhere, and hunger, and water, and rain, and being wet. Floating on anything that could float. I do not like to think about the flood. I like to think about dry land. I like to think about song. Do you remember the songs of the oafs, little brother?"

Then he and Mike had sung the old songs, after which he said: "There aren't too many of us left. The mans are wiping us out."

"Yes they are. But that is because we were not wise stewards of the earth. And so the great creator has given the world over to them. One day we shall all be gone."

And again the great pinhead knit up his brow. "Yes. It is too bad. But aren't the mans making the same mistake by wiping *us* out? Are we not children of the great creator too? When we are gone, will not great nature miss us?"

Mike could find no answer for him, and thus they parted that day.

Mike would recall the big oaf fondly as a great singer of songs, for he knew all the old songs. Mike would also recall him as a great poser of questions, for he would pose questions that Mike had no answer to.

From time to time, Mike would encounter other oafs (or *giants*, as they were now called), and the oaf would say to him, "Little brother, why do you dwell here among these mans?" and he would angrily shout, "What does it look like I am doing? I own them! They are mine! Stay away from my mans, pinhead!"

Thus, Mike protected his village of mans from the occasional wandering oaf that was looking for an easy meal, for oafs in their feral form are territorial and do not encroach on another oaf's land, even if he is a *shorty* who stands just under ten feet.

Mike was married three times and well outlived each wife each time, for the year of the oaf is three times the year of man. He fathered forty children, each of whom was tall, but not so tall as to be mistaken for an oaf.

Each of Mike's children had red body hair and faces full of frecks.

Most of Mike's 308 grandchildren had red body hair and frecks also, though not all of them. Many, but a little fewer than most, of Mike's 3,402 great-grandchildren had red hair and frecks. Mike's great-great-grandchildren numbered well over 60,000 and their descendents made up a large part of the village-states of Reddberg, Roseberg, and Mikelberg, and a sufficient number had red hair and frecks and lofty physical statures, but not all.

Ultimately, the world of mans grew and the world of oafs shrank. There came a day when mans began to hunt oafs for sport. Indeed, the head of an oaf became a trophy of great value and worth more than its weight in silver, for the mans did learn to love silver as their world grew.

And when the day of death came for Mike, who never did change his name to Tlotl, he was the last of the oafs, for the mans had hunted them into absolute extinction, man being an excellent and natural hunter.

Oafs, who were once thought to be gods, were never seen in the world again.

And the songs of the oafs were heard no more.

—The End—

APOCRYPHA

I shall not be slave to silver, nor banner, nor king—be he king of the west or king of the east.

—Great Scripture

Sing oh Sing of Great Lord Uulf

And the bard did sing:

In ancient days there was an oaf of great renown sent to the eastern tribes from the great creator above because they were pious and did follow the tenets of great scripture.

And Uulf, son of oaf and angel, ventured into the dark provinces of the west seeking after their wenches of fairest countenance.

When two oafs of the west were sent out against him, he slew them both with one hand.

And then four were sent out against him and he slew all four with his two hands.

And then six were sent out against him and he slew all six with his two hands and a foot.

And then eight were sent out against him and he slew all eight with both hands and both feet.

And they asked themselves, What are we going to do about this? And they sent out ten and he said, Well, I'm all out of limbs. Now I must unsheathe my sword.

And so he did. And they all fell. All in all, on that day he slew thirty oafs of the west, twenty with his hands and feet and ten on the point of his sword.

And he dwelled among the tribes of the west for forty days. He reveled among them and made trouble by day, and at night he frolicked with their wenches. And in between he played the songs of the east on his wing-ed harp, for he was a great lover of music.

And no oaf among them dared to lift the sword against him though he insulted them by singing songs of love for the tribes of the east while in the halls of the west.

And when Uulf finally returned to the east, the great King Hrdrada said to his lords, I have never seen an oaf mighty like this! Bring him to me. He shall lead our armies to victory against the west. Did I hear correctly that he slew thirty while dwelling among them?

But when he came before the king, he told them, No, I shall not slay an oaf for silver, nor banner, nor king, unless it pleases me.

But we are at war, cried the great king. If we do not fight we shall be enslaved by the west.

Then fight your war! Uulf answered. But I shall not be slave to silver, nor banner, nor king—be he king of the west or king of the east. This war began before I was born and it shall be here at my end.

He would not hear another word from the great king, and he began to play his wing-ed harp, for as you know, he was a great lover of music.

He played to his delight, and no oaf among them dared lift a sword against him though he insulted them by playing the songs of the west in the royal palace of the east.

And this insult angered the great and crafty King Hrdrada. In his wrath he whispered to his lords, If Uulf won't go to the war, we'll bring the war to him.

And the king ordered his lords to bring the war to Uulf's house. During a bloody skirmish when the soldiers of the east saw the tide of battle turning against them, their lords ordered them not to surrender, but to retreat to the village where stood the house of Uulf and his old mother.

When the noise of battle awoke Uulf, he quickly hid his mother under a bed. Then he unsheathed his sword and went outside.

Uulf slew 144 on the point of his sword. When the soldiers of the west saw what was happening, they made a hasty retreat.

And the east cried, With Lord Uulf leading us we are assured of victory, for he is mighty in battle.

And they rewarded him with five shield bearers, ten luf'tnts, a hundred female mans to be sacrificed, a hundred wenches of fairest countenance, and a thousand pieces of silver.

But he immediately released the luf'tnts of their obligation to him and he sent them back into the war under other lords;

Likewise, he released the shield bearers and he divided the female mans among them and ordered that they not be sacrificed, for he was a lover of mans;

He also released the wenches of fairest countenance and divided five hundred pieces of silver among them;

He gave the remaining five hundred pieces of silver to his mother.

And he told the crafty and great King Hrdrada, I know what you have done, and I am wise to you. I know it was you who brought the war to the house of my mother. I know that you are implying a threat to her life if I do not do as you ask. I understand that I cannot always be there to protect her from your eternal wars and from you. So I shall do as you ask and lead your armies of the east in battle by day. However, I shall sleep in the houses of the west at night.

And Uulf led the soldiers of the east against the west by day and did slay many, but he slept in the houses of the west at night.

And there was nothing that anyone could do, for Uulf was sent by the great creator and his strength and valor were without equal on earth.

And here the bard did end his song.

Great Lord Uulf Is Brought Down Low

And the bard did sing:

The king of the west, Olentzlero, was brother to the king of the east, Hrdrada. Olentzlero was greatly troubled by Uulf's insult to him and to his brother, as well as his frolicking at night, which corrupted the morals of the young. Now, this king was wise in his ways. He sent a lord to the house in the west where Uulf slept at night with his wenches. The lord, who arrived with a company of ten oafs, said to Uulf, Come with me, for the great king has a gift for you.

Uulf followed him to a cave. When he went inside the cave the lord and his oafs quickly rolled a large stone to block the entrance. They heard a great noise inside the cave in which they had hidden a great heagle and a great snake. Now this, they said, is the end of Uulf. But after the noise of battle had ended, Uulf pushed away the stone and emerged from the cave wearing the feathers of the heagle as a hat and the skin of the snake as a belt.

He told them, Thank your great king for his gifts. I find them much to my delight.

Then he slew the lord and his ten oafs with his sword.

The next day, he wore the hat of the heagle's feathers and the belt of the skin of the snake; and leading the oafs of the east against them, he slew a hundred in battle.

The next night the dark king sent a lord to the house wherein Uulf slept with his wenches. The lord said to Uulf, Come with me, my friend, for the great king has another gift for you.

Nodding, Uulf followed him and his company of twenty to a cave. When he went inside the lord and his oafs rolled a large stone to block its entrance. They heard a great noise inside the cave wherein they had hidden a great wulf and a great beo. Now certainly, they said, he cannot prevail against a wulf and a beo. But after the noise of battle had ended, Uulf pushed away the stone and emerged wearing the fur of the wulf as shoes and the fur of the beo as a cloak.

To the lord he said, Thank your great king for his gifts—now I have a cloak and shoes to match my hat and belt.

Then he slew the lord and his twenty oafs at the point of the sword.

The next day he wore the shoes of the wulf's fur and the cloak of the beo's fur along with his hat of the heagle's feathers and his belt of the snake's skin, and he slew two hundred more in battle.

The next night the dark King Olentzlero sent another lord to the house in the west wherein slept Uulf with his three immoral wenches. The lord said unto Uulf, Come with me, if you dare, for the great king has another gift for you. This lord had a hundred oafs with him.

Uulf followed him to a dark cave. When he went inside the cave the lord and his oafs rolled a large stone over its entrance. And they heard a great noise inside the cave in which they had hidden a beautiful wench with poison in her mouth. When they rolled away the stone they discovered that the noise was the miserable cry of Uulf.

I went to kiss her, Uulf said, and she spit in my eyes and now I am blind. Tell your king he has brought down great Uulf!

And here the bard did end his song.

THE DEATH SONG OF GREAT LORD UULF

And the bard did sing:

King Olentzlero had Uulf put in chains and made him a slave in the west.

By day he would grind corn in their mill, and by night on a perfumed bed of feathers he would grind in sacred union with the king's hundred daughters.

Many paid ten pieces of silver to watch his grinding by day. And they played furious music on the wing-ed harp as they laughed.

A hundred pieces of silver was paid by a select few to watch his grinding by night. And they played furious music on the wing-ed harp while they marveled.

The great creator came to Uulf in a dream. Will you not fight in my army, my child? he said.

Uulf answered, But they have made me blind, lord.

When you had eyes, you could not see, the great creator said. It is I who have made you blind so that you can see. Open your eyes and tell me what you see.

Uulf opened his eyes within his dream and said, I see an army of wenches greater than all the armies of the west, and they have enslaved your people.

The great creator said, These are the daughters of King Olentzlero, who carry your seed, an army that will grow up to enslave my people.

Uulf understood the dream and he said, I will fight in your army. I am your warrior.

When he awoke from the dream, evening had become night and the hundred daughters of the king had come to him to be grinded. He grinded them indeed. He grinded them with his hands until each was dead and his seed within her.

Only one daughter escaped and cried out for the soldiers of the west to come quickly.

Uulf, though blind, reached out into his darkness with hands that were guided by the great creator and he slew a hundred of them.

They called for one hundred archers, for after seeing that, no oaf dared approach him.

The archers let fly one hundred arrows, ninety-nine of which hit their mark, but Uulf was not undone.

And when the hundredth arrow hit its mark, Uulf, the son of oaf and angel, earth-son of the great creator, breathed his last breath.

It took one hundred arrows to slay him, they marveled. Indeed, he was the greatest of the great creator's warriors.

All in all, in his lifetime of battles against the west and revelry, Uulf slew more than 5,000.

And here the bard did end his song.

Life Song of Great Lord Gerwargerulf

And the bard did sing:

The girl who was not slain with her sisters by Lord Uulf's righteous hand, Grietjel, the firstborn daughter of Olentzlero the Mighty, king of the west, gave birth to a son who grew to be an oaf of great size, the tallest oaf on earth because an oaf had given birth to a child of Uulf, the earth-son of the great creator.

Gerwargerulf was a monstrous monster, this boy, but brave and strong. He became a lord in his grandfather's armies two years before his full maturity because he was an oaf of great valor and strength—the strongest ever, after Uulf.

Like Uulf, he was a lover of the wing-ed harp. He practiced on it all day when he was not in battle—and he was a ferocious warrior who killed hundreds of oafs from the east single-handedly.

And there came a day after a battle in the east that the giant oaf dismissed his soldiers and went alone to a small hill to think about songs to play on his wing-ed harp, for this was his true passion, not war, which he only did as an occupation.

While he was deep in contemplation, Gerwargerulf heard a child's voice. The boy was singing a song so sweetly!

When he peeped over the hill, he saw a boy of about eight dressed in the garments of his enemy the east.

The boy was there with a girl of about the same age, who was also from the east. He was singing to her a song he must have composed, for on occasion he would change a phrase and ask her if she liked it better that way.

This went on for some time until Gerwargerulf heard the boy amend a phrase that was excellent and he blurted out: No, child! Keep it the way it was before!

The two children from the east looked up and saw the awful head of Gerwargerulf. He was twice the size of any oaf they had ever seen. They quickly got up and ran away, fearing for their lives.

Monster! Monster! they screamed.

This made Gerwargerulf very sad, for he was a sensitive oaf, a true lover of music, and he did not wish to be feared.

For the rest of his life Gerwargerulf kept the boy's song in his head and always wondered whether the child had settled for the better phrasing or the lesser. From time to time, he would hum the boy's tune and modify it to his liking.

He told himself: This war will be over soon and when it is, I am going to find that child and sing to him my version of his song. I am certain he will like it, for I have improved it in a way that honors his heart song!

Gerwargerulf would imagine the boy from the east and himself traveling the earth together as musicians.

It was four years later, so the boy would be about eleven, maybe twelve.

At that point Gerwargerulf had killed over three hundred oafs of the east, though as a sensitive lover of peace, he had mourned every death as a great loss to oafenkind.

At long last there came a day when he was called into a meeting with the lords of the west and they told him what he had waited so long to hear: The war will be over tomorrow.

A delighted Gerwargerulf said, Are you certain? How is this to be accomplished?

Well, music boy, they kidded him, it will be over with the death of one small oaf.

A delighted Gerwargerulf prodded, How? Tell me how.

They said, You will engage in battle tomorrow against a champion from the east. His name is Wiftet and the enemy claims that he is a fierce warrior blessed by the great creator with great gifts. However, our spies say that he is a mere boy with no great gifts at all.

We believe that the east is weary of war and they are sending the lad to be sacrificed so that it might end.

You, great son of Uulf—music boy, they laughed good-naturedly—have been chosen to do the honors.

Make it a good kill, they shouted, for king and creator!

A good kill, a delighted Gerwargerulf echoed, for king and creator!

On the day of the battle, Gerwargerulf was dressed in full and resplendent armor.

He had a broadsword, a tall feathered helmet with visor, and a stately shield bearer who bore his mighty shield.

Trumpets blared as the oafs of the west gathered behind their giant champion.

Then trumpets on the opposite side of the battlefield blared as the champion from the east appeared, and the oafs from the west did hoo and haw in their laughter.

Indeed, it was a small boy—an oaf of eleven, maybe twelve, wearing no armor but a tunic of war so large for him that it gathered at his feet and dragged on the ground. In his hands were his weapons: a few smooth whispering stones and a sling.

Gerwargerulf cried aloud: How pathetic! They have sent a boy with pebbles to pester me! He's no bigger than a little man man. Come, then, little man man. Come and taste of death!

He had a good belly laugh as the boy with the handful of pebbles began to run toward him.

Everyone on the west shook with jibes and laughter, while everyone on the east held a collective breath.

Great Gerwargerulf raised his great sword and thundered in his gait toward the boy.

One last death, one last good kill, and this war will be over, thought the great oaf Lord Gerwargerulf, and then his ears picked up something.

The boy was singing.

It was familiar music. It was the song!

This was the boy who had composed the song!

Gerwargerulf halted his charge and lifted his helmet to get a better look at the boy.

Indeed it was he! Wiftet was the boy! Oh what a great day!

In his joy, Gerwargerulf, the player of the wing-ed harp, was not reminded that he was in battle.

But Wiftet, the little singer of songs, did fit a smooth whispering stone into his sling and let fly.

As Gerwargerulf was shouting most joyously, You are the boy that I have been longing to see! the whispering stone guided by the hand of the great creator struck him in the forehead a mighty blow, which cracked his monstrous skull.

The giant oaf Gerwargerulf, the greatest oaf who ever lived, collapsed to his knees, teetered for a moment, and then fell forward into the earth.

Cheers rang out from the east and died away into the vacuum of stunned silence on the west.

But Gerwargerulf was not dead yet, only dying, for when the boy Wiftet went to him with the sword given to him by the king of the east to sever the head of the giant, he heard these words that no one else could hear:

Bend down low and listen to me, great singer of songs.

And little Wiftet bent down low, and these were the words the dying Gerwargerulf said to him:

I am he who frightened you that day by the hill, but I was only trying to hear your beautiful heart song.

Live long, music boy, and give much music to the world.

For the world needs the goodness of song.

Kill only if it brings peace as my death has brought peace.

And thus did die the greatest oaf who ever lived.

The great Gerwargerulf.

Thus did die the son of mighty Uulf, earth-son of the great creator.

Lord Gerwargerulf, the only one and the last one of his kind.

The great singer of songs, Gerwargerulf.

And little Wiftet did sever great Gerwargerulf's head with the sword given to him by King Hrdrada.

And the forty-year war between the east and the west came to an end at last.

And all oafs were again united as one tribe under one standard.

And when little Wiftet grew up and became king, a period of peace and prosperity did follow, the likes of which has never been seen before nor since, for he did rule with the goodness of music in his heart.

And when Wiftet died, his twin sons Euphus and Wiftet the younger battled over the royal seat, and there was war, for the earth was again divided into halves and ruled by two brothers with opposite ideals.

It has been this way ever since.

And here the bard did end his song.

Harp Song 104

There is a flower, a common flower, and they all pass it by;

There is a flower, a common flower, with only a thousand, upon a thousand, just the same;

There is a flower, a flower most rare, on the side of a high mountain, and they climb, they climb the mountain, to pick the flower most rare;

They fall, fall from the mountain, to their black graves below, but they climb, climb the mountain, to get the flower so rare;

At last they get, get the flower, the flower that is most rare, and they clutch, clutch the flower, it is a beauty so rare;

The flower, the flower, the flower is love, and it is a beauty so rare.

—Great Lord Gerwargerulf

I Do My Goodness Do

An oaf am I, and I cannot change, but I do my goodness do;
And my brother says, He is evil, can't you see?

And I do my goodness do, and goodness comes back to me;
But when they ask my brother he says, He is evil, can't you see?

I plant the seed in season, and feed the hungry and the poor,
I bless my friends with kindness, and forgive my enemies.

And when I ask my brother he says, You're not evil, can't you see?
When I ask my brother he says, I am evil, Can't you see?

When I ask my brother he says, I am jealous of you.

—A folk song from the Forty-Year War; Attributed to King Wiftet; but attributed by King Wiftet to Lord Gerwargerulf (King Wiftet affirms these are the corrections to his song that Lord Gerwargerulf whispered to him as he lay dying)

Three Little Man Mans

Once upon a time in the Village of Mans, there lived three little man mans who were of the same litter and so they were brothers.

And in the morning the littlest man man went to cross the bridge to go to the field where the trees were ripe with the sweetest fruit.

But as the man man crossed the bridge, there came a loud oafen voice that rumbled up like thunder from a deep pit, a voice so mighty that the bridge shook as the oaf spoke: "Where do you think you're going, little man man, on my bridge?"

The little man quaked as he answered: "I'm going to the field to eat the ripe fruit."

"No you're not," said the mighty voice.

"Why not?" asked the quaking man.

And the voice answered, "Because I'm going to eat you!"

A mighty oaf came up from under the bridge and grabbed the quaking man in his hands and opened his great mouth to eat him.

The little man man pleaded desperately: "Please don't eat me, great oaf. I'm really too puny to eat. In a few moments my brother will pass this way. He is much bigger than I and will certainly make a more satisfying meal."

The oaf smiled at this, for he was very hungry indeed and could use a more satisfying meal than this puny, little man man. And so he released him into the field, then he ducked back under the bridge to wait for the big brother.

Just as the little man man had promised, in a few moments his big brother did arrive, and the bridge did shake with the mighty voice that thundered: "Where do you think you're going, little man man, on my bridge?"

The second man man, who was quite a bit larger and more delicious looking than the first, quaked as he answered: "I'm going to the field to eat the ripe fruit."

"No you're not," said the thundering voice.

"Why not?" asked the man as he shivered with fear.

"Because I'm going to eat you!" cried the mighty oaf as he came up from under the bridge and grabbed the shivering man in his hands and opened his mouth to feast upon him.

"Please don't eat me, great oaf," cried the shivering man. "I'm really too puny to eat. If you are patient, in a few moments my brother will pass this way. He is much bigger than I and will certainly make a more satisfying meal."

"Another brother? Even bigger than you?" said the great oaf, licking his lips.

So he released the little man into the field and ducked back under the bridge to wait for the big brother.

Sure enough, in a few moments, just as the little man man had promised, his big brother did arrive. And he was a very big man, indeed, for the bridge above the oaf's head did tremble as he set foot upon it.

The oaf was so hungry he could not wait anymore and he jumped up onto the bridge.

But the big man on the bridge was riding a gallant hoss and wearing heavy armor. He had a long spear, a quiver full of arrows, and a broadsword, which he did heft with ease.

As soon as the oaf saw him he ducked back under the bridge, but there was no safety there. The man hurled his spear into the oaf's neck, which brought the clawing, crying creature back up, and he filled his great breast with arrows shot from the bow with a strong and sure hand. When the horrid creature fell, the man finished him off with one mighty swoop of the sword and gave the great oafish head to his little brothers.

It was quite a treasure.

MIKEL

The woman next to him on the bus was trying not to, but she was staring.

That was okay. Mikel was used to people staring.

She noted his freckled, pudgy cheeks, the prepubescent twinkle in his eyes, the brick-red book bag with stickers of cartoon characters on it, and finally asked, "How old are you?"

The beaming boy, who quite enjoyed the attention, looked down at the woman and said, "I'm nine, and I'm going to see my father. I have to take three trains and four buses to get there. He lives very far away. In Mapleton."

"That is very far away," the woman said. "Where is your mother?"

The boy explained, "Because of my height, I can travel alone. No one will trouble me."

"Indeed, you are very . . . tall for your age," the woman responded. "You'll be okay, I'm sure, but I'll keep an eye on you until you change buses."

"Thank you very much. I will enjoy your company," the boy said, digging into his pocket. "Would you like a stick of gum, ma'am?"

He held out his enormous hand and the tinfoil-wrapped stick of gum floated like an insignificant strip of silver on a vast ocean of pink palm. When she took it from him she marveled at how small her hand was compared to his. Her hand was not even half the size. And how uncomfortable he looked with the large knees of his long legs pressed against the back of the seat ahead of theirs.

Despite all that, he was still beaming, and he was talkative as most children are at that age. Somewhere amid his chatter, he informed her, "I am the tallest boy in the world, you know?"

"I believe you."

Indeed, Mikel was the tallest boy in the world according to the *Guinness Book of World Records*, of which he had two copies, a paperback which he carried around with him in his brick-red book bag to show people when they stared, and the hardcover which he kept on the desk in his bedroom opened to page 321.

He was the tallest boy in the world at 6'10" and he would probably grow taller with the years. At nine, he was three inches taller than Robert Wadlow was at that age, yet he was not the tallest boy who *had ever lived*. That distinction belonged to his father, whose somber black-and-white photograph stared back at him from page 321 of the *Guinness* on his desk in his bedroom. When his father was nine, he had already reached the lofty stature of 7'7".

His father was the tallest man who ever lived, though Mikel had never met him.

His mother had always told him, "There were some difficulties, as you can imagine. He is very shy. He does not like people very much. The stress of all that got to him and we separated. But he is a good man. As you can see, we live very well. He's very generous with his money, and he never forgets your birthday."

In the crease between pages 320 and page 321 of the *Guinness* was the photograph of the infant Mikel in the arms of his smiling father.

"He loved you very much and was proud to be a father. That's why he is smiling," Mikel's mother would explain.

In the photograph his father had rust-colored hair shaved close to the scalp and a long curly beard of a slightly darker red. Between these parting crimson whiskers, there was the smile. It was the only photograph of the hundred or so that Mikel owned of him in which his father smiled. As far as he knew, it was the only photograph in the whole wide world in which his father smiled.

Mikel had never seen his father's smile in real life, but that was all going to change because his father had called yesterday with a message: "I want to see you. Every boy should know his father."

When Mikel changed buses, he sat next to a new nice woman, who stared and said, "You're very—"

"Tall for my age," laughed Mikel.

On the trains it was the same thing: "Tall . . . for your age."

"Yup," said a beaming Mikel, offering gum all around until he ran out. When he ran out, he offered breath mints. He was a very gentle, very friendly child, and people reacted to him with both amazement and kindness.

On the final bus, the one that took him into Mapleton, Mikel was plumb worn out and he rested his head against the back of the seat ahead of his and fell asleep. He awoke and looked up and saw that the bus driver had come back to his seat and was shaking him.

"This is your stop, kid."

"Thank you, sir. I'm going to see my father."

"I know," said the bus driver. "I've met your father a few times."

Mikel was eager to hear more. "What's he like?"

"He's big."

"Oh." He already knew that.

He got off the bus in Mapleton, a small community way up in the hills. There weren't too many houses, but everyone he encountered seemed to know of his father, seemed to know immediately that he was the son of his father, and pointed him in the right direction.

His father lived in an immense Tudor mansion overlooking a cliff. It was gray with black trimmings. In the yard maple trees grew in abundance like a well-manicured forest, and here and there daisies and hollyhocks bloomed in patches.

The main door of the estate was left open and built high enough to allow entrance to a man of great height, and Mikel skipped delightedly through it.

Inside, Mikel giggled. No bumping of his head would go on in here—the ceiling was high enough! The grand paintings on the wall were at a level with his eyes so that he could enjoy their magnificence without stooping or stepping back to view them. There was ample space between the furnishings so that his wide hips and big feet could move about comfortably without knocking things over. All the chairs and tables were sturdily built to accommodate his great height and weight.

Mikel had never had it so good.

For the first time in his life he felt like a normal-sized kid. Giggling madly, he ran from chair to chair, plopping down and testing each for comfort and bounce.

When he caught sight of his father at the entrance to the main room, silently watching his antics, he froze.

"Sorry."

"Don't be," said his red-bearded father in a voice that casually boomed from his slightly parted lips.

Mikel's jaw dropped. His father looked to be head and shoulders above him. He had to be sure, so he rose from the chair, and even standing, he had to look up to see his father's face. His father was over nine feet tall.

"You're so . . . tall!" Mikel exclaimed.

"Yup." His father embraced him and lifted him as easily as any father would his nine-year-old child.

"Daddy," Mikel said and began to cry into his father's chest. He had so many questions. There were so many things he needed to know. And now, at last, they would all be revealed to him.

His father said, "There, there, son, do not cry. Your patience has been rewarded. Every boy needs to know his father. Now wipe your tears away and I will tell you all you need to know. I will tell you the story of my mother and my grandmother, and of my stepfather Jack and my real father the oaf, and you will learn the meaning of your great height and mine. I will tell you of a land of silver. I will tell you of the small singing harp of gold. I will tell it to you as my mother told it to me when I was younger than you are now and shedding many tears because I did not fit in. It begins in a place far, far away, but not too far at all. It begins with a boy who had a man . . ."